Praise for *How to Outrun a Crocodile When Your Shoes Are Untied*

A *Los Angeles Times* Summer Reading Pick!

"Debut author Keating delivers a fun-filled, pitch-perfect book... Humor, poignancy and fascinating zoological facts infuse the narrative with a warm conversational tone... An amusing, highly readable book about the perils of being twelve in a snake-eat-snake world."

—*Kirkus*, starred review

"An absolutely perfect summer read."

—Girls' Life Magazine.com

"As if junior high isn't enough of a zoo, Jess Keating's debut...[is] a menagerie of laugh-out-loud antics and relatable tween woes."

—Anna Staniszewski, author of *The Dirt Diary*

"A wild romp, filled with humor and heart."

—Lisa Schroeder, author of *It's Raining Cupcakes* and the Charmed Life series

HOW TO
OUTSWIM
— A —
SHARK
WITHOUT A
SNORKEL

JESS KEATING

sourcebooks
jabberwocky

Published by Sourcebooks Jabberwocky, an imprint of Sourcebooks, Inc.
P.O. Box 4410, Naperville, Illinois 60567-4410
(630) 961-3900
Fax: (630) 961-2168
www.jabberwockykids.com

Library of Congress Cataloging-in-Publication data is on file with the publisher.

Source of Production: Versa Press, East Peoria, Illinois
Date of Production: October 2014
Run Number: 5002738

Printed and bound in the United States of America.

VP 10 9 8 7 6 5 4 3 2 1

Also by Jess Keating

**How to Outrun a Crocodile
When Your Shoes Are Untied**

To the brave kids, the weird kids, and the cool kids. Especially the ones who don't yet realize they can be all three.

I love the smell of the universe in
the morning.

—*Neil deGrasse Tyson*

Really, Mr. Tyson? *Really?* What about the smell of hippo poop wafting into your bedroom window in the morning? Or the wet-dog stink of a flock of pelicans who strut around like they own the place, and no matter how often you try to shoo them out of the way, they get even more puffed up and snooty at you? I don't know what your universe smells like, but around here, my universe isn't exactly the sweetest smelling peach in the pie. I mean, not that I blame you or anything, and I don't mean to sound rude. Just...you know? I'm too busy trying to keep up with my own little life to pay attention to what the universe smells like.

Sorry for snapping at you there. No hard feelings, okay, Neilio?

Chapter 1

Some sharks can never stop moving, or else they will suffocate and die.

—Animal Wisdom

whoa, sucks to be them! Can you imagine never getting to sleep in? Or laze around on a Saturday morning in your jammies watching cartoons? But they can grow like a zillion teeth, which would probably come in handy for eating jawbreakers and scaring mean people. So maybe it evens out in the end.

Hijinks at the Zoo?

August 20

Visitors to Denver's Zoological Park and Gardens this Sunday got a big surprise when Ana Wright, granddaughter of the famed Shep Foster, fell into a shark tank during an educational presentation. The twelve-year-old was not injured.

"It looked like she threw herself in!" said Jonathon Wexley, a local business owner who witnessed the accident. "One minute that other girl was talking about sharks, and the next? She just jumped!" The impromptu dip in the shark tank wasn't the only surprise that day, when police arrived at the scene to arrest

One month earlier

Throwing myself into a shark tank is *not* my idea of a good time. Luckily, my summer didn't *start* with sharks. But it did start with some big changes.

No. Big is an understatement.

Ginormous.

Über.

Behemoth.

It also started with a crocodile chomping down on my finger.

Good thing she was only six inches long, huh?

"Ouch!" I yelped, yanking my hand away from the teensy snapping jaws. "She got me!" I inspected my finger, searching for signs of blood. Her pinprick teeth didn't break the skin, but there was a row of teeth imprints that looked like a zipper on my finger. The little bugger gawked up at me with her taupey-yellow eyes. Almost as if she were trying to say, "Who, me?! I'm too *cute* to hurt you!"

Please. Reptiles can't fool me.

The babies had hatched only minutes ago, just in time for Grandpa to call us at home in a frenzy, giddier than a dog in a Milk-Bone factory, yammering on about "the miracle of life" and all that. From what I could tell, the miracle of life came with a lot of...*goo*. The hatchlings were already chirping up a storm and nipping at fingers when Daz and I got there. That's the thing about living in a zoo. You've got to be ready for *everything*.

And right when you think you've got things sorted out, it up and changes on you all over again. Sometimes there are even crocodiles there to *remind* you not to get too comfortable, because life will go biting you again.

Think I'm joking? Let's recap the past month's highlight reel, shall we?

Top Three Changes in My Life

1. My entire family now lives in a zoo. And I don't mean that in the dramatic, metaphorical sense either. Although my twin brother, Daz, is an absolute monkey. More on him later. I used to think living in a zoo would be crazy, but it turns out I actually LOVE it. Well, parts of it. You know, once you get past the whole poop thing. I especially like giving educational presentations like my mom, but that *definitely* took some getting used to.

2. My best friend, Liv, lives a billion miles away, in a place called New Zealand. For a while after she moved, I didn't think I would be able to survive without her, but I'm trying to stand up for myself now, which is actually a lot harder than it sounds.

3. I have a grandfather. Okay, that's not exactly big news, but my grandfather is *different*. Instead of playing chess and wearing old-timey knit sweaters like most grandpas, mine follows dangerous animals on television and wears Hawaiian shirts. Oh, he's also dating a supermodel actress named Sugar. It's his fault that exactly 3.4 million people have now seen me on the Internet giving my presentation about reptiles at the zoo.

4. My room smells like hippos.

Wait.

Did I say there were only three things? That's what happens when you live in a zoo. Your brain gets all scrambly like eggs in a pan.

I placed the feisty croc baby back in the incubator next to her sisters, giving her the "how dare you bite me?!" stink eye for good measure. The large plastic tub was filled with craggy wet eggshells and crocodile goop.

"Watch yourself, there!" Grandpa chuckled. "We don't want you losing a finger."

Daz made a face. "She's *fine*," he said, rolling his eyes.

CREATURE FILE

SPECIES NAME: Daz Ridiculosis

KINGDOM: Currently the third bedroom of our zoo house, which smells suspiciously like moldy cheese, gym socks, and stale Cheetos. How can he *live* in there?! The place should be declared a biohazard zone.

PHYLUM: My Idiot Brother (Despite my attempts to get Mom to admit he's adopted, apparently we are actually twins. But not the kind that look like each other. Thank God for that.)

WEIGHT: Still 120 pounds of sarcasm. Some things never change.

NATURAL HABITAT: Sneaking around the zoo, spooking tourists; the bathroom (how else will he get his spiky hair to defy gravity like that?); hanging out with his best friend Kevin who *happens* to be the most adorable guy on the planet.

FEEDS ON: Cheetos, my annoyance, and the hoard of snakes he keeps as pets.

LIFE SPAN: Pretty sure he's a robot.

"It's not like they can do much damage," Daz said. "Why do they sound like squeaky toys?" He held a crocodile baby gently in his hands and lifted it to his face, grinning. "This one looks like she's smiling! Look! I should take her home and call her Daz Jr.!" He started cooing, baring his teeth at the reptile.

It grinned back, confirming my theory that Daz shares a brain with all cold-blooded creatures. Any minute now he would convince them to do his bidding and there would be an uprising.

Grandpa picked up one of the leathery eggshells, turning it over in his hands. "They're calling for their mother," he explained. "In the wild, they even chirp like that *inside* their shells. That's how the mom knows they're almost ready to hatch. Sometimes she'll even help them hatch by rolling the eggs around in her mouth."

I frowned, trying to get that slimy image out of my head. Thank God *humans* didn't lay eggs.

"How long do we get to keep them?" I asked. "You said they're going somewhere now?" I reached in and scratched my little biter on her scaly head.

Grandpa nodded. "They'll be on their way soon!" He set the eggshell back into the incubator and wiped his hands on his bright red Hawaiian shirt. "We were helping out with a breeding program for research, but they'll need forever homes now that they've hatched. Great news for the species!" His eyes twinkled the way they always did when he was talking about animals.

A pang of sadness skipped through me, knowing these cute little creatures wouldn't be around here for the summer. It's not every day I get to hang out with reptiles that *can't* chomp my arm off, you know?

"Hey," Grandpa said, noticing my frown. "Buck up! Besides," he said, waggling his eyebrows mysteriously. "Don't forget about my little surprise! You'll have *plenty* of chances to have fun this summer, with or without these little guys."

My breath caught as tightness grew in my chest.

I know normally the thought of surprises made kids happy. But can you blame me for being a little weirded out? The *last* time Grandpa surprised us, I ended up living in a zoo and got humiliated on national television in an interview that I'm positive will put me on a therapist's couch one day. I wasn't sure if I could stomach another patented "Shep Foster surprise." I could only hope it didn't come with a camera crew this time.

I tried to look excited, or at the very least like I wasn't dreading what he had planned. "Are you sure you can't just *tell* us what's going on first?" I ventured. "It's not like you need to surprise us all the time. We're not little kids anymore." I glanced at Daz for support, but he was too busy trying to fit his new crocodile BFF in his shirt pocket to notice.

"I'm going to make her a bow tie," he announced, ignoring our conversation.

Well, *I* wasn't a little kid anymore.

I still wasn't sure what Daz was.

Grandpa tsked me. "Nonsense! One of a man's biggest joys in life is surprising his kids and his grandkids! Your ol' grandpa doesn't have many surprises left!" He nudged me with his elbow, doing his best to look pathetic and pouty.

Oh, please.

I don't know about other grandfathers, but mine

could dodge rattlesnakes and make homemade rafts from bamboo and dental floss if he needed to, so the whole "let-a-poor-old-man-have-his-fun" routine wasn't working on me. "Seriously! I could even help out if you told me! Ugh, *Daz*, you are not taking that thing home with you so get it out of your pocket!"

Grandpa helped Daz untangle the crocodile's mini claws out of the fabric of his shirt as she chirped in irritation.

"Tell you what," Grandpa said, crossing his arms over his chest. "You can help out by going home right now and getting the four bags that are hidden in the front closet and bringing them by the polar bear tank in exactly ten minutes."

"Ten minutes?" Daz perked up. The promise of a surprise was enough to make him forget his plan to smuggle out reptiles. "We get our surprise today?!" He started bobbing up and down with trademark Daz excitement.

Grandpa laughed. "If your sister here can get a move on, *yes*!" He checked his watch. "You'd better hurry, actually. Party starts in about ten minutes, with or without you!"

I grinned. Despite being a total wackadoodle, Grandpa could be pretty fun. "Okay!" I said. "Four bags. Front closet. Polar bears!"

Grandpa narrowed his eyes, wagging his finger

at me. "And *no peeking*!" he added. "I mean it! I'm trusting you! That's why I'm not sending the Dazmanian devil here," he muttered, slapping Daz on the back.

"Yeah, yeah," I said, sticking out my tongue. "Promise!"

I waved good-bye to the crocodile hatchlings and headed out the door, feeling that anxious buzz of excitement that seemed to follow me around everywhere lately. Grandpa had first mentioned his surprise for us a few weeks ago, and despite our complaining, he'd actually managed to keep it secret. It was totally out of character, which made me even *more* nervous. Was it a trip to Hawaii? A new documentary he was starring in? Maybe he'd commandeered a spaceship and we were all going to spend a year on Mars.

Even my *parents* didn't know what was up.

Hurrying home, I dodged the throngs of people milling about our yard. Our house was supposed to look like a decorative research station built near the lion pen in the African Pavilion, but to us, it was home for the summer while my parents did their research.

I was rounding the zebra pen when someone shrieked, her high-pitched voice echoing over the swarms of visitors. I whirled around at the noise.

"Hey, it's her!" A little girl pointed from a water

fountain, her face lighting up like I had a "free ice cream" sign. "It's Ana Wright! That's her! *Hey, Ana!*"

Two young girls rushed toward me. They waved madly while their mother snapped a picture. "Ana! Can we get a picture with you?" Their flip-flops slapped against the ground as they hopped in place.

I panicked, imagining what the pictures would look like. *Not with this hair! Not in this shirt! Gah, is that crocodile goop on my shoulder?* But the smiles on their faces were infectious. I forced myself to stand taller, digging inside for my bravery.

"Sure," I said, waving them over to stand beside me. *Just be cool.* I reached back to tighten my ponytail, hopefully pulling my style from "crocodile nanny" to something closer to "human almost-teenager." I wished for the zillionth time that I looked more like Sugar, my grandpa's superhot girlfriend.

The girls looked about six or seven, both with shiny red cheeks from the hot sun. A green bag overflowing with gift shop stuffed animals was slung over their shoulders, and their zoo T-shirts were baggy on them. Their lips were stained with what looked like red Popsicle juice. Life was so *simple* when you were a little kid. Not like the nonsense I had to put up with.

"We loved your presentation last month! I want to be you for Halloween this year! I got a hat from the gift shop and *everything*!" The girl with strawberry blond hair was practically panting she was talking so fast. She dug into her bag and pulled out a crumpled hat, tugging it onto her head. "How cool is it that you're going to be in an actual *movie*?!"

I smiled for another photo but felt the strain in my cheeks. "More like a documentary," I said, gripping my nails into my palm. "But it is definitely crazy!"

There's an understatement.

It had been a few weeks since I'd been a part of the media circus at the zoo, filming my presentation for one of my grandpa's documentaries. Because of all the press about it, I was still getting recognized by some people. This is one of those ginormous changes I was talking about, and boy, was it taking some getting used to. Getting recognized in school was one thing. But while I was out wandering around the zoo? That's some level ten bizarro right there.

"Is it true that you're named after an anaconda? And that you're the youngest presenter here?" The one with black hair stared at me with wide eyes. She lowered her voice. "I read that online," she whispered. Her sister nodded wildly.

I tried not to cringe. "Y…yes," I said. A month ago, I wouldn't have been caught dead admitting that, but they both beamed.

"We know everything about you," she said solemnly.

Yikes.

Hopefully they didn't know I had to wear my old Wonder Woman underwear today because I'd forgotten to add my laundry to the pile like Mom had asked me last night.

That'd be awkward.

"What's with all the construction signs, huh?" the girl chattered, pointing over to the polar exhibits. "We ran into some by the bears. Are you getting some new animals?" Her face lit up. "*Ooh!* Are they going to be part of your next presentation?! Are they pandas?! I *so* hope they're pandas!" The girls were bouncing again on their heels.

I backed away slightly. All that energy was hard to handle, you know? Like they were sparking firecrackers about to go off.

"Uh," I said. "I'm not sure. It's been super busy this summer so far, but I don't know if we have any new animals coming," I admitted. "It's a lot of work to get new creatures here, so it only happens after a *lot* of planning."

"*Ohhh,*" they said together, their mouths dropping open with awe. I checked my watch. My time was running out, and as nice as the girls were, I *really* wanted to find out what Grandpa had planned. I glanced up to their mom hopefully.

"All right, girls," she said, giving me a conspiratorial smile. "Let's not take up too much of Ana's time. She probably wants to enjoy the rest of her day! Say thank you!" She coaxed the girls away as I waved good-bye.

"Bye!" They waved one last time as they left, babbling happily on the way.

I wiped the sweat from my forehead and kept marching home, marveling at how much my life had changed.

You wouldn't think there would be a really big difference between being twelve and being twelve and a half. Doesn't look like much, right? Just that one little half.

Turns out, that little half can make all the difference in the world.

Last month, I was the most anonymous person on the planet. Okay, that's not exactly true. More like I *thought* I wanted to be anonymous. Invisible. If I could have zapped myself down to the size of an ant, I would have done it before you could say "elephant poop." Sometimes, I still catch myself wanting to hide and be anonymous, but if there's one thing the last month has taught me, it's that being brave enough to be your true self takes *work*. You can't suddenly say "Ta-da! I'm brave now!" and be done with it.

Totally sucks, right?

Darwin was perched on top of his living room cage when I opened the front door. He's my African gray parrot, and despite being a total loudmouth, he's still one of my best friends, so as long as he behaves, I like to let him out to explore. He even lets me practice my presentations in front of him and gets excited when I talk about reptiles. You should have seen his face when I told him he was related to dinosaurs. Total drama queen.

I yanked open the front closet, digging through the coats in search of Grandpa's secret gift bags. It was no wonder Mom hadn't found them yet—this closet looked like a war zone, with winter hats and scarves stuffed in every cubby and opening.

"Well?" I spoke to Darwin as I searched. "Any ideas on what the surprise is? Now is your chance."

He ruffled his feathers and shuffled into his cage, tempted by the tray of grapes and seeds I'd left him this morning.

"Suit yourself," I said. "Ah, here we go!"

Four bright blue gift bags were tucked against the back wall of the closet. Lifting one by its handle, I swung it gently, trying to judge the contents by the weight like I do at Christmas. It was superlight, and the only sound it made when I shook it was the crunching of tissue paper that popped out of the top. I glanced out the front window to check for nosy visitors.

I could have one look, right? A teensy peek?

Darwin's squawk scared the bleep out of me. "Okay!" I yelped, nearly dropping the bag. "I won't cheat!"

Giving him a mega-glare, I bunched the handles of the bags together in one hand and headed for the door. "Don't get mad at me if Grandpa is getting us all *cats*!" I hissed at him on the way out.

It was a good thing Grandpa hadn't sent Daz, because there was no way in Santa's snowy workshop that he would have avoided the temptation of looking.

Just saying.

When I made it to the polar bear exhibit, my parents were waiting outside with Daz and Grandpa. My doubts about Grandpa's surprise grew as I saw that they looked as confused as I felt. I checked around us for the press, but no suspicious people with cameras were lurking nearby. Honestly, it's like Grandpa *liked* messing with my nerves.

Mom whipped around. Her hair was messy, frizzing out around her hat. "Ana! We've been waiting for you. Dad wouldn't start without you." Her wild eyes told me she was as on edge about all this as I was. The back of her zoo uniform was stained with perspiration.

"I brought these." I set the bags down beside

me as Grandpa noticed me and clapped his hands together. Sugar stood beside him in her usual miniskirt and heels, wriggling with excitement. (She had on a shirt too, but something about eight miles of leg made it hard to notice that.)

"We're all here!" Grandpa cleared his throat, and I could tell a speech was coming on. He *loved* to have everyone's attention. A few zoo visitors lingered around us, watching inquisitively. "As you know, I've been planning a little something as a surprise." He turned to look at Mom. "Janie, you remember that summer we spent on that fishing boat? When you were six or seven?"

Mom nodded, but she was still wary. She took my hand and gripped it tightly. "Yes…"

Grandpa smiled. "Well, I've been thinking, a little time at sea should be mandatory for all kids." He gestured widely with a faraway look in his eyes.

I did not like where this was going.

"Dad…" Mom said. Her voice was low. "What did you do? You know we can't send the kids on some boat right now."

Boat?! Who said anything about a BOAT?!

"Mom?" I said, panicked. I squeezed my nails into her hand, communicating my terror. Beside me, Daz was practically bouncing out of his skin.

Grandpa shook his head. "No, no, no," he said.

"There's no boat this time, although that *would* be a great plan." Sugar nodded sagely but kept her lips pursed.

Already I was feeling seasick.

"*But* I did manage to wrangle some resources together. *Secretly*. Which is very hard to do around here, I'll have you know." He winked and led us toward the construction signs behind him.

Dad glanced nervously at me, tugging at his mustache. We followed behind Grandpa slowly, like he might lead us into a lion's den. Which, knowing him, he totally would.

"And I'm very happy to report that it has been a success," Grandpa continued. "We're not completely finished with the renovation, but we're going to go public soon. I wanted you to know first, before Sugar and I leave for Los Angeles again tomorrow."

"Know what, Shep?" Dad said. Always the voice of reason. His eyebrows were scrunched together.

"Glad you asked, Henry," he said. "Why don't you open your presents first?" He lifted his shoulders and giggled innocently.

The paper crackled as I numbly handed out the bags, keeping one for myself. Digging through to the bottom, I felt something hard and rubbery. Then some sort of long…tube?

Whaaa?

"Snorkel gear!" Daz erupted, tossing his bag to the floor. He waved a black-and-blue snorkel mask and stuck the snorkel in his mouth. "Fee gof ufs shnorkul fgear!"

I stared at Grandpa, dread sinking deeper and deeper into my stomach.

"Now you're ready," Grandpa said, corralling us closer to the building.

He threw open the plastic tarp around the pavilion door, and we all stepped inside. The first thing that hit me was the cool air.

Well, that and the fishy smell.

Chapter 2

Jellyfish have existed for more than six hundred and fifty million years.

—*Animal Wisdom*

Guh, they obviously didn't have any famous grandparents planning surprises for them, because I'm pretty sure the stress of all that is cutting down my life span.

"Ta-daaah!" Grandpa sang out.

Mom and Sugar gasped. Daz wheeled around to gape at the ceiling, and Dad stumbled back a step, bumping his head into a display of sculpted exhibit rocks.

I blinked at the bright light. We were surrounded

by Caribbean blue walls with a mural of sharks, rocks, and jellyfish painted all around us. Glass tanks and silvery gray rocks flanked us. A plastic sign was mounted above us, the letters hanging at odd angles.

"The Marine Adventure Zone," Daz read aloud. He turned to Mom. "What's that mean? Ooh, are there sharks in here?!" His eyes widened with excitement as he ran up to the shark anatomy paintings on the wall.

"Not yet!" Grandpa said, giggling like a little boy. "But soon!" He reached up and adjusted the sign. "Still needs a bit of work obviously, but I wasn't able to keep it a secret from you any longer," he explained, beaming. "What do you think?"

Mom rubbed her hand over one of the tanks. "'Adventure Zone' meaning what?"

"The zoo has been wanting to introduce some new interactive exhibits for a long time, and when I saw how great Ana was doing with presentations, and remembered how much *you* used to love our boat trips, I knew it was the right thing to do," he said. "This is a place where kids can come and interact with real live marine species. This tank here will be full!" He gestured to a low horseshoe-shaped tank along the left side of the room.

"Real sharks?!" Daz shrieked. My stomach flip-flopped as I stared warily at the painted sharks on the wall. Even their fake painted-on teeth looked scary enough to me.

Grandpa waggled his eyebrows. "One hundred percent real," he said. Then he noticed the uneasy look on Mom's face. "Safe ones, mind you. Every animal here will be safe for kids of all ages. Manta rays, some gentle sharks, and some jellyfish, sea horses, and octopi in the side exhibits." He pointed to the side walls, which had built-in tanks incorporated around the rocky exterior.

I stared up at Mom. I wasn't exactly sure what this had to do with *us*. But maybe Mom was just his inspiration, like he said? My shoulders drooped with relief. This could be sort of...*cool*.

"Wow, Dad," Mom finally said. "This is...great. Really! What a wonderful addition to the zoo." She reached over to hug him. I had to admit it, having a touch tank seemed like a super-fun idea for visitors. So long as they didn't have any man-eating sharks here. I eyed the biggest tank suspiciously.

Could a great white fit in there?

"And the best part is that Ana and Daz can join in the fun!"

Say what?

Beside me, Daz hooted with glee.

Grandpa shrugged. "It seemed only fitting to have the zoo's youngest up-and-coming star at the helm of this ship! Why do you think I got you the snorkels? So you can play the part! Daz can learn some of the natural history, and Ana can work the crowd with her dazzling wit!"

I gripped the side of the tank beside me. I may have wit, but it's definitely not dazzling. Maybe more of a dim sparkle.

"Wait," I said, the realization crashing over me. "You want me to talk about sharks?"

"Not only *talk* about them!" Grandpa said. "You get to have fun too! You can hang out with the sharks and help the visitors!"

No, no, no, no, a million times no to the sharks.

"Surprise!" Grandpa said.

Now that's the understatement of the year, right there.

"Dad," Mom interrupted. "We've only recently gotten Ana acclimated for her presentations with the reptiles. I think she should stay where she's most comfortable." She blinked at me nervously and she kept her voice low and controlled. "You remember how difficult it was for her."

I cringed at the memory. The panic attacks. The hot spotlight that felt like it was going to singe my skin. The look of pure joy on evil Sneerer Ashley's face when I *almost* messed it up in front of everyone.

I pointed at Mom eagerly. "Yeah! What she said!

I'm acclimated! It was *difficult*!" Even though I had no idea what *acclimated* meant, I knew that it sounded right. Really I was thinking, *Nope, not changing plans now, nope, nope, nope.*

"Oh, come on, Janie! You know she'll love it!" Grandpa said. "Who wouldn't love to spend a summer working with sharks right here?! It's hot outside, and it's *cool* in here! Plus, it's mostly kids in here. She will be great to help them interact with these animals. It's perfect!"

I shook my head. "But no! I want to stay where I am! With the reptiles! I'm the crocodile girl, remember?!"

Okay, so that wasn't exactly official or anything. But more than a few people had nicknamed me that, so why confuse them, right?

Right?

Daz piped in. "What? Are you afraid of them or something? Come *on*. It's sharks!"

"No!" I hissed. The heat crept up onto my cheeks despite the cool room. "I just like animals with… legs," I said feebly, avoiding everyone's eyes.

It wasn't actually the sharks that bugged me. But why would I want to change things now, when they had finally started to feel okay? What if I *hated* being with the sharks? Who would I get to work with? What if they didn't even like me and spent all day trying to bite me? The sharks, I mean, not the people. What if I started having freak-outs again because it was a new place? My old, scaredy-cat self was clawing its way out of me. What if—

"Well, I've already told Patricia you'd be great for the job. She's in charge of the new species and said she would love the help. I can tell her you'd rather stay where you are, if you want to," Grandpa said. He wrung his hands together and gave me a pouty look.

Great. I'll take panic with a side of guilt, please.

Mom sighed. "He was only trying to surprise you, Ana. We really did have a great time when I was a kid." She squeezed Dad's hand. "You might love it," she said. "You won't have to be *in* the tanks the whole time either. It's more of a fun thing to do while you learn. Then you can lead your talks as usual. Only this time about sharks. You don't *have* to do this. But maybe you should think about it…?" Now it was Mom's turn to give *me* puppy dog eyes.

Ugh. More guilt.

I peered around at the fake rocks and my family. Everyone, even Dad, looked like they were ready to dive into some super-happy pool of summer fun but couldn't do it with me holding them up, dipping my toe in the cold water.

That familiar clammy, tight feeling of fear choked at my throat, threatening to take over…

No.

I forced myself to stand straighter. If things were going to keep on changing like this, then I would just have to find a way to figure it out and deal with it without going all hot-jittery mess like I used to. I would *adapt* and change however I needed to, like Darwin (the scientist guy, not my parrot) was always talking about on the evolution posters in the Natural History Pavilion.

I *refused* to let something as simple as man-eating sharks scare me.

Okay, that's a bad example.

I set my jaw. *Adapt, Ana.* "Okay," I said. "I'll do it! Fine! Yes!" Nervous laughter bubbled up inside me as a proud smile burst onto Mom's face. She squeezed my hand, and my shoulders relaxed as I leaned in for a hug, but the squirmy feeling of doubt seemed to smirk at me from the inside.

I shoved the feeling down as Grandpa pulled me into a tight hug. "Yay, Ana Banana! It's going to be great!"

I took a huge breath and smelled the salty ocean tang in the air. My heart was lighter already, buoyed from the pride of not letting my fear ruin the day again. All I needed to do was make sure my bravery didn't run off and hide like a dog from a bath with all these changes going on.

Maybe this wouldn't be so bad?

Five Things about Summer That I Hope NEVER Change, No Matter How Many Sharks Grandpa Throws at Me

An "Ana Will Stay Positive" List

1. That feeling of the hot sun beaming against my back when I get out of the pool that feels like a giant hug. And since it's summer, the days are extra long, almost like the sun *knows* it should hang out a little while longer in the sky instead of hightailing it below the horizon like the rest of the year.

2. The taste of ice-cold lemonade mixed with a teensy bit of iced tea that you can hear when you drink because of the *clinky-clink* of all the ice cubes against your upper lip.

3. That toe-stretchy feeling of waking up late in your cozy bed, knowing that no matter *what* happens today, you don't have to go to school and take a math test.

4. Getting to stay awake as late as I want, without having to worry about the alarm clock waking me up early in the morning. *Technically*, Mom and Dad only let us stay up a little later, but instead of turning off the lights and threatening to ground us like they do during the school year

when they catch us up, now they sigh and shake their heads and say we'll be sorry in the morning. Yeah, right!

5. Never *ever* having to see the Sneerers, especially their ringleader, Ashley, who devotes her entire existence at school to ruining my life. Okay, probably not her entire existence. But if her existence were a root beer float (another awesome summer drink), the root beer would be how much time she spends on preening, the ice cream would be how much time she spends wandering the mall with her minions, Rayna and Brooke, and the fluffy foam on top would be how much time she spends trying to mess with me. So. Extra nice to not have to worry about her for two precious months. If I could handle Sneerers, I could definitely handle sharks, right?

Chapter 3

The scarlet skunk cleaner shrimp cleans
other fish of dead skin and parasites. Some
fish even let it clean the inside of their
mouths without harming it.

—*Animal Wisdom*

Blech! GAG ME.

"Turn around! I can't see your butt!"

"I don't like it!" I ducked away from my computer
screen with my hands over my backside. "The fabric
sticks out funny, and it makes my butt look big!"

"You don't *have* a butt, so how is that even possible?!" Liv glared into the webcam and spun her
finger in the air. Her voice sounded tinny and faraway, but her eyes were bright. "*Turn around!*"

CREATURE FILE

SPECIES NAME: Liviola Hobbitonius

KINGDOM: Far, far away from me, living with the hobbits in New Zealand.

PHYLUM: Supersmart Girls Who Are Also Lucky Enough To Have Hair That Always Looks Good; Best Friends Who Moved Away

WEIGHT: Considering how much junk food she eats, I'm pretty sure she's 80 percent sugar.

NATURAL HABITAT: Hard to tell now, seeing how I haven't seen her in person for months.

FEEDS ON: Our video chats, musical theater (especially anything with singing boys in old-timey costumes), and as much red licorice as she can get her hands on.

LIFE SPAN: She's technically in another time zone eighteen hours ahead of me right now. Does that mean she's living in the future?!

HANDLING TECHNIQUE: Best friend since first grade, when I dropped my toast on her (grape jelly side down, no less). No special techniques needed.

Even though she'd been living in New Zealand for the past couple of months, that didn't stop Liv from helping me with my wardrobe choices. Before she moved, Liv and I used to spend *hours* on the phone and at each other's houses. We even talked to each other on the phone at the same time as we'd chat online. But now it cost an arm and a leg (so said Mom) to call her, so Liv and I had been using the computer to video chat.

It worked okay most of the time, except for the time when Daz heard us and gave me fake moose antlers from behind my back, which Liv thought was hilarious, but *honestly* brothers are the worst.

"Arggh, *fine*," I said. "Happy?" I backed away from the screen and spun quickly, slamming my arms against my sides. "See? Funny butt."

Liv's eyes widened, and her lip curled up in false disgust. "You weirdo. You look fantastic! It doesn't make your butt stick out. It makes you look like you *have* one! It's a miracle! It stays in the keeper pile."

I slumped down into my chair and tugged the fabric lower against my knees. I still wasn't used to all of this. When I decided I couldn't spend my whole life squirreled away trying to pretend I was anonymous, I knew I'd have to make some changes.

So far, tackling the "image" part of being my true self wasn't very helpful. Really, I needed a new wardrobe. But since I didn't have any money, I was getting rid of all the clothes that made me look like a ten-year-old, including my favorite *Peter Pan* T-shirt with the hole in the armpit, even though it was *so-o-o* comfortable.

Okay, I might have kept that one. But I promise not to wear it in front of people, okay?

"But it's so short!" I said. "Are you supposed to see my thighs like this?" I squished a finger into my leg, watching as the skin turned white, then slowly left behind a reddish fingerprint.

Technically I didn't pick out this skirt. Sugar bought it for me last week, but I think she forgot that I would be wearing it instead of her. Unfortunately, I look less like a model and more like a twelve-and-a-half-year-old who's got a weird pickle-shaped sunburn on her knees.

Liv lifted her eyebrows smugly. "Trust me. It stays in the keeper pile. Kevin will love it! How is it going with him, anyway?" She disappeared off screen and returned with her mouth full. Her cheeks stuck out like a chipmunk.

I shrugged. "It's fine, I guess." I squinted at her. "Liv, it's practically midnight there. What the heck are you eating?"

She grinned, showing off the mess in her teeth. "Izza eez an eat fie!" she mumbled.

I raised an eyebrow. "Oh, well that makes it clear."

She swallowed her bite. "It's a cheese and meat pie. They love these things down here. Pies for breakfast, pies for lunch. Pies, pies, pies," she sang. She took another big bite and held it closer to the screen. "Want fum?"

I scrunched my nose and stepped out of the view of the computer, slipping out of the skirt. Once my robe was pulled on, I sat back down. My skirt sat in a pile on the center of the floor, like a swishy black hole that was sucking out my ego.

"Okay. So quit changing the subject now," she said, leaning back in her chair. "Tell me how *Kevin* is. Has he put the moves on you yet?" She giggled like a madwoman, her eyes shining like giddy little pixels on my screen.

I frowned. "I told you! He's fine. We all had a good time at the dance, and he's coming over later to hang out with Daz. So he's fine. I'm fine." I shut my mouth before I rambled too much.

"The 'fine-itis'? Come on. You're a terrible liar. Your lips always do that thing when you lie." She squinted at me, squishing up her lips.

My hand whipped to my face. "What thing? They do not!"

She smirked. "Sure they do! You think in a lifetime of best friendship I don't know your lie face?

You do this." She pursed her lips together again, sticking them out like a duck. "You look like you're slurping spaghetti when you lie!"

"Okay, *okay*!" I yelled. I made sure my lips were loosey-goosey. "I guess I was sort of confused about the dance."

"Because he didn't tell you he loved you and give you a giant smackeroo on the lips?"

"No!" I said. I hid my lying lips. The truth was I was sort of afraid of kissing him. Or anyone, really. But that didn't make me stop wondering if *he* wanted to.

"I just don't know what he's thinking, you know? I hate that feeling." I stared at Liv's face on the screen. "We did slow dance four times. That counts, I think?" I thought back to the dance and how Kevin had gone to get me punch like guys in the movies do for their dates. "Maybe he only sees me like a friend?" I said.

"Leilani says that when a guy likes you, he will make sure you know it," she said. "Maybe he's working up to it?"

I rolled my chair away from the screen, making a face. *Leilani* was Liv's new friend, and I couldn't help but get a little peeved when I heard her name.

Lay-lah-nee.

They met when Liv moved into her new house,

and she plays the flute and never seems to care that she's yanking my very best friend away like some sort of kraken. So I've never actually met her and she *could* be a perfectly nice person, but still. Liv was *always* talking about Leilani's opinion on stuff, like she was somehow smarter than us just because she had purple hair and was like eight months older.

I returned to the screen, plastering on my best "Leilani's-name-doesn't-bug-me" face.

"Maybe, yeah." I poked aimlessly at my spacebar, trying to clean it. There had to be easily two years' worth of toast crumbs in there.

"Plus, he got you that totally sweet present before your zoo thing, remember?"

My eyes slid over to the notebook that Kevin had given me before my presentation. I had been so nervous to be in front of people, but he had shown up to surprise me in his supersweet way and said I'd be great. I still hadn't written in it; it was too perfect. I liked it better blank, full of possibilities.

"Maybe that was only as a friend, though? I got you presents all the time when you were still here." When Liv used to live up the road, we used to give each other little gifts like flowers or used books or special flavors of lip gloss. My heart hurt to think about it.

"That's true, but I am pretty awesome." She

fake-primped her messy hair. "Leilani's already kissed a guy. She said it was super sloppy, and that he was super drooly like a dog. I think as long as you kiss someone by the time you're in high school, you're good."

I bit my lip. High school used to seem so far away, but now it was almost close. Only one year away. It was hard to imagine someone else's *mouth* anywhere near mine. Did it feel like kissing your pillow? Not that I'd ever done that. Except that one time in sixth grade when Liv and I had that sleepover and watched *Pride and Prejudice* on the Women's Channel. Even though I didn't think that Mark Darcy guy was *that* hot.

Although he did have quite nice hair. And I liked how he was super serious but also sweet to Elizabeth at the same time.

I wasn't sure if I wanted a kiss. Maybe I did? Did the squirmy feeling in my stomach when I saw Kevin mean that I did? Or did it mean that I was a total freakazoid who didn't have the first clue about the opposite sex?

Ugh.

See? I can't even *think* that word without feeling weird. Even though it's totally scientific and not at all gross.

"Oh!" Liv exclaimed suddenly. "How could I

forget to tell you? Guess what happened yesterday!" Her eyes widened and a happy-sneaky look appeared on her face, like she was about to scarf the last handful of theater popcorn from the bag.

"Umm…you ran into a real live hobbit?" I ventured.

"Nooo." She beamed. "Even better. Hang on. I'm going to *show* you." She dashed away, leaving her empty chair spinning behind her. It was hot pink and squishy looking, instead of the green one she had when she had still lived here. I guess it would have been hard to pack stuff like chairs with a big move like that. It was weird seeing her in a new chair, somehow.

She came back, waving a letter in front of her. "Check it out!" She unfolded the paper and tried to hold it steady for the webcam.

"I can't read that," I said. "The letters are all blurry."

"It's my transcript!" she squealed. "My parents were talking to the school board guy yesterday. You know, checking up on my classes to make sure I'd be okay here in their school system for the winter start."

"Yeah, and?" Oh man, it would be awful if Liv got held back a year. Were they supersmart in New Zealand? What if they were way ahead of us with lessons? I held my breath, ready to give her a pep talk.

"I get to *skip a grade*!" she squealed.

A cold fist gripped my heart. "You...what?" I sputtered. This wasn't right.

"Yes!" She grinned. She held her transcript to her chest. "They said I was too advanced and that I would be bored in eighth grade here, and their school system is different here with classes, and all the extra work I did to catch up for the move, and...I get to start *high school* this year! How cool, huh?!"

My eyes blinked uncontrollably. "Wow," I managed to say. My throat was tight. "That's...insane. I thought we'd be going into high school together," I said. I couldn't keep the disappointment from my voice. "I mean, together, in different places. Obviously." My face was hotter than the Serengeti.

Liv didn't notice. "I know! I was so excited when I found out. That means I get to go to classes with Leilani too. I was all worried that I'd be stuck alone in some class full of people with weird accents that I don't know."

"Yeah. That would suck," I said.

Almost as bad as it would suck for me to go back to junior high while you're in *high school*.

I felt about two inches tall. I never realized it before, but I always sort of felt like Liv and I were reading the same book, you know? Like, the book of *life* or something, which sounds totally nerdy, but true. Now, instead of being on the same page as me, she was flipping ahead a few chapters, leaving me stuck in the dust like a tiny footnote. How was this fair? And how come she wasn't afraid at all? If I found out I had to go to high school this year, I'd be pulling out my hair and rocking in a corner. What would I wear? Who would I talk to? You need *time* to get used to big stuff like this. And here's Liv flouncing into ninth grade like it's no biggie.

I was just starting to get used to everything without her. Being in school without her. Eating vanilla shakes at Shaken, Not Stirred without her. How come after trying so hard to be okay with my life, things had to go changing again? First the sharks and now Liv.

"Earth to Ana? Did you hear what I said?"

I snapped back to reality. "Huh? Sorry, no…" My eyes were stinging, but she probably couldn't tell from the pixelly image.

"Our pact! Remember? We need to fast-track it!"

I stared at her face on the monitor as I tried to remember. Pact? Liv had already missed the half-birthday pact last month. What other pact was there?

"Um," I said, trying not to hurt her feelings. "Right."

"Our kissing pact!" she squeaked. "We only have a month now instead of a full year!"

"Oh!" I exclaimed. A dark feeling crept over me. Like a snake winding itself around my heart.

Oh.

See, Liv and I *had* made a kissing pact, back when we were eleven years old. This was when everybody in school started talking about kissing for the first time, but Liv and I weren't really interested. We always told ourselves so long as we kissed a boy by the time high school started, we wouldn't have to worry about being labeled as losers for the rest of our lives. We made a blood pact to do it together too, using a safety pin to prick our pointer fingers and smush them together like they do in the movies. My finger hurt for hours afterward.

"But *I'm* not the one going to high school!" I fumbled. "Why do I have to kiss someone?" My voice sounded higher than I wanted, and I could see by my little picture in the corner of the monitor that my ears were bright red. I flipped my hair to cover them.

"Duh! We have to do this *together*, remember!" she said. "Since I'm starting high school in the fall, we have to go by *that* time line! It only makes sense! Because that's the only way we'll get to keep the pact! It's *logic*, Ana!"

I considered this. It sort of seemed to make sense. But it didn't *feel* that good. Mainly because the thought of having to kiss someone this summer felt like someone shoving me onto a roller coaster without telling me. How was I supposed to do this without any preparation? I'd thought I had a full year to get ready.

"You're practically ready now with Kevin. Besides, you don't want me to have to kiss someone *alone* this summer, right?" Liv whined.

"No!" I said. But inside I was screaming, "*Yes!*" How come Liv didn't seem freaked out about this shorter deadline? Did that mean she was more ready to kiss someone than I was? Did she already have someone *picked out*? I mean, yeah, if I *had* to kiss someone, I would definitely pick Kevin. He's a million times better than *Zack*, even though my binder from last year has Zack's name scrawled all over it with little hearts, but that's only because I was a royal dimwit back then. But could I picture kissing Kevin *now*? *Gah.*

"Good." She relaxed. "So we'll both get kissed this summer or have our eyes be eaten out by worms?"

I never did like that part of the pact, but we had watched a gross movie on the Scream Channel that night so it had given us the idea.

"Yes," I said firmly. "First kiss this summer. No biggie." I shrugged like I wasn't completely mortified.

God, I am such a liar.

"So what's this business you were saying about sharks and your grandpa?" Liv asked. By the way her smile curled, I could tell she had no idea I was secretly flipping out on the inside right now. I *hated* feeling like we were growing further apart, even with little things like reading each other's minds.

I opened my mouth to answer, but suddenly, the last thing I wanted to do was chat. I was afraid the truth would come spilling out of my mouth and she'd never let me live it down. I feebly knocked on the underside of my desk with my fist. "Oh. Hang on, Liv." I swiveled in my chair, pretending my mom was at my door. "Okay, Mom," I said to no one.

I turned back to Liv. "Sorry, I have to go. Mom wants me to help out with dinner." I rolled my eyes, like I was upset to hang up. I couldn't remember a time when I *didn't* want to talk to Liv, ever.

"Sure, no problem! Talk later!" I held my smile as she waved good-bye and disappeared with a blip. I let my breathe whoosh out of me. Normally after talking to Liv I felt like I could do anything. Like I could take on the world. How come this time, I felt like I'd been hit by tsunami?

Was it normal to feel bad after talking to your best friend?

Chapter 4

The blue whale is the loudest animal on earth, with a whistle that can be heard for hundreds of miles underwater.

—*Animal Wisdom*

Huh. I always thought Daz was the loudest animal on earth.

Whoosh! Whoosh! Whoosh!

The water circulation system in the Marine Adventure Zone sounded like a gigantic gurgling heart as I leaned up against the fake rocks mounted onto the wall.

It had been almost a week since we'd found out Grandpa's surprise, and now the tanks around me were full of crystal clear water, with printed pictures of who would be living in them stuck to their sides. Epaulette sharks, sea horses, manta rays, and even some species I'd never heard of before. The animals hadn't arrived yet, but I could practically hear them taunting me. What would it be like to be a shark and not have to worry about kiss pacts?

"Hello, Ana!" Patricia popped out from the back room. I'd seen her around other exhibits before, but this was the first time I'd met her. A small sense of relief spread inside me as she shook my hand. She was older than my mom, but she had a kind smile and a small turtle badge that glittered on her chest. "So happy to meet you finally! Shep has told me all about you. I heard about your crocodile presentation last month. Congratulations!"

The cell phone clipped to her belt buzzed, startling her. "One sec, kiddo," she said, turning to face the sea horse tank. "Patricia speaking. What's up?

"Uh-huh," she continued. "Yep. No, she was hoping to show up today, but I got a call last night saying she couldn't make it."

A pause.

I watched her talk, noticing how frizzy her hair was. She was like a poodle with a perm in this humidity. I smoothed mine down, just in case.

"Oh? Well, that's great!" she said. "I'm starting with Ana right now."

My ears perked up. I gave her a questioning look.

"Sure," she said. "Send her on over. I can talk with both of them."

She hung up the phone and clipped it back to her belt. "Well, good news! You're going to have some company in here!"

"Someone who doesn't mind toothy sharks, I hope?" I touched a picture of a nurse shark against the tank, flattening out the edges.

Patricia laughed. "You bet! We've had a great response from schools since your presentation last month. Many parents have called to see if their kids can help out as volunteers in different areas."

My heart lifted. "Oh yeah? That's cool," I said. Surreal too, that people were paying any attention to me at all.

"Is the new person a student then?" I was hopeful. Patricia seemed okay, but it might be nice to have someone else my age to hang out with while I was in here. I felt a stab of sadness that Bella couldn't have joined in with me here, but she was so busy with her new historical cooking classes that she barely had any spare time.

"Yup," she said. She dug into her pocket and pulled out a crumpled paper. "From your school too!" She reached to the top of her head for her reading glasses and settled them onto her nose.

My mouth went dry as I tried to remember what kids I knew who might be interested in hanging out at the zoo. Kevin? *If only.* Maybe it was that girl with the braces who always drew ponies on her notebook?

"Um…let's see here…what was it again?" She flipped through a stack of papers from her pocket. "Annalise…? No, that's not it. Andrea? Addison? *Hrmm.*" She clucked her tongue. "I know it's in here somewhere. I should really know before she shows up and I mess up her name," she muttered. "Right! Here it is! Ashley! Her name is Ashley!"

My hand slipped against the side of the tank and dipped into the frigid water below.

Ashley?!

I dried my hand on my shirt, blinking fast.

There was no way. Absolutely no way that prissy, perfect-haired *Sneerer* would volunteer to work at the zoo surrounded by messy animals. There was bound to be some other Ashley at our school. Even though I couldn't think of a single one. That girl who always wears a braid and reads romance novels in the cafeteria? Was her name Ashley?

I tried to wipe the mortified look off my face before Patricia thought I was seriously unhinged, but the rustle of the plastic tarp by the pavilion door made me whirl around. A young girl stepped inside.

A girl with arched eyebrows, pink-painted toenails, and a very, *very* familiar sneer.

"Hello, *Scales*," Ashley said.

I couldn't find my voice. Obviously it was hiding somewhere now, cowering from the Sneerer beside me.

Speak.

Speak! I commanded myself like a dog. I couldn't let her think I was scared. I had to say something.

Patricia clasped her hands together. "Excellent! Glad you found your way here! Ashley, this is Ana. Ana, Ashley." She made the introductions as Ashley blinked at me. Every lash taunted me. "Looks like you two already know each other! That will make your time here extra fun."

Ashley grinned. "For sure! Ana and I go way back, don't we?"

I gaped at her. "What are you doing here?" I wanted to sound like I wasn't completely mortified. But...*what was she doing here*?

She shrugged. Her shoulders glinted in the light with some shimmery bronze powder. Or maybe her skin was naturally super sparkly? Maybe she was a vampire that fed on human fear?

"What? A girl can't want to help out at her local

zoo to get summer credit? You know we have to volunteer somewhere. I thought the zoo would be *perfect*." She held her hand out and examined her nails. Probably making sure they were sharp for when she sprang forward to attack me like a leopard.

Assertive. Confident. Sophisticated.

Pick one, Ana.

"Sounds like you two have a lot in common," Patricia said happily. "Let me grab you some introductory forms. I've got them here in my binder somewhere. This place is such a mess!" She bustled to the other side of the room and knelt down by the big shark tank. "Forms, forms, forms," she muttered, while Ashley stood there, rigid like some angelic statue.

I took the chance. "You can't be here." I kept my voice low. "You *hate* this stuff. It's animals. And stinky. And *work*. Remember what happened *last* time you came here…" I glared at her. Finally some of the fire in my stomach was growing.

I didn't need to be scared of Ashley. I'd already shown her once this summer that she shouldn't mess with me. The whole thing was still lodged firmly in my brain as one of my scariest moments ever. It was my first big educational presentation in front of everyone, and what did Ashley do? She tried to mess me up *completely*. I'm talking smarmy stares, evil laughs, and *she* was the one that got my whole class invited to watch. She even had her little harpy friend Rayna film it so she'd have *evidence* when I panicked.

So I taught her a lesson.

And she deserved it.

I mean, it wasn't exactly *my* fault that Frankie went to the bathroom all over her sandals during my big presentation in June. And it wasn't my fault that camera crews were there to film it for my grandfather's movie, which got national coverage on all the major television news stations. And it wasn't my fault that for the first time in Ashley's life, people laughed at *her* instead of me.

Okay, maybe it was a little my fault. I *had* handed her the croc in the first place.

But she had it coming.

She clicked her tongue. "You're not the only one who can work, you know." She stretched her arms over her head, yawning. My skin crawled at the thought that she was getting comfortable here. This was *my* space. Suddenly I wanted to work with the sharks. Anything to show her this was where I belonged and where *she* didn't. I wanted to grow a tail and turn into Ariel if it meant she would leave me alone here. This was my chance to adapt and prove to myself I wasn't destined to be fighting against my scaredy-cat ways forever.

"But why here? If you're going for volunteer credit, why don't you just work at an old-age home?" I blurted, but willed myself not to feel small next to her anymore. I had to stop this awful thing she did to me, making me feel like I was turning into a crispy, dead leaf that was going to crumble away in the breeze. I had to remember how it felt when everyone was on my side, and *she* was the laughingstock instead of me.

My next words felt like fire on my tongue. I darted a glance at Patricia to make sure she wouldn't hear. "I'm sure there are tons of places in the *mall* that will take you."

She sniffed, still holding her smile. But I could see it wavering at the sides. "It's none of your business why I'm here," she said. "All that matters is that you can't stop me." Her words slowed as she drew out the next sentence. "And you, *Ana*"—she grinned happily—"are going to have to deal with it."

For some reason, hearing her call me my real name was even scarier than when she called me "Scales." I wasn't about to tell her that, though.

I shook my head. "Fine. You won't like it here, you know." I knew I was right, so how come I could already feel my insides unraveling like an old sock that was being torn apart by a lion?

She nodded, her blond hair shifting on her

shoulders like a bunch of silky yellow snakes. Medusa with better accessories.

"Whatever." Her eyes darkened. "I'd be worried about yourself, not me."

Something stirred in my chest. Is that why she was here? Was she trying to sabotage me?

Suddenly the room seemed to shrink, and my safe, awesome place to be myself felt foreign and menacing. Nobody would believe Ashley if she said something awful about me here, right? This wasn't *school*. She had no power over me here.

But I couldn't get my stomach to stop churning.

"Why can't you just leave me alone?" I sputtered.

"What makes you think this is about you?" she spat.

"Ready to get to work, guys?" Patricia was back with our forms. "You're pretty lucky that you know each other. I bet all the other volunteers here are working together for the first time!" She laughed in her jolly way. My eye wouldn't stop twitching.

Ashley nodded readily. "I know, right? *So* lucky." She beamed and then, horror of horrors, wrapped her tanned arm around my shoulder. Her manicured nails dug into my skin.

"Great! Let's get you started. You can hang out in here if you want, but the most important thing is that you learn about each new species we're going to be housing. I've printed off all the information you need, so why don't you go over it and start to quiz each other on some of the natural history facts? There are pictures on each tank of all the animals too, so you can get used to where they will be. Ana, you normally work with the reptiles, so most of this will be new to you too, so you can learn together. This way when the new animals show up this week, you'll be up to speed."

She smiled widely, and I could tell she was trying to make Ashley feel welcome. Like laying out a welcome mat for the devil. Next she'd offer her cookies.

"Sounds great!" Ashley cooed, grabbing her forms and tucking them under her arm. "Ready to go, Ana?" She raised her eyebrows expectantly.

What.

Is.

Happening?

Chapter 5

Three meters long and spiraled, narwhal
teeth used to be mistaken for unicorn horns.
—*Animal Wisdom*

Didn't people used to think unicorn horns had
magical powers? Maybe if I wrangled myself a
narwhal tooth, I could use it to cast a spell on
Ashley and turn her into a mealworm.

So I've figured out that if we lived back in the olden
times, Ashley would probably get burned at the
stake as a witch.

I know. That's pretty morbid. But it's Bella's
fault, having all these books about medieval people
and how they were all treated *really* badly whenever
they ticked off the royals.

Actually, it would make more sense that Ashley would be royal back then. Because wouldn't that just be the way of it? And then *I* would probably be the one to get tarred and feathered, all because she lifted her royal finger and declared me a "pox on our land!" or something else super-medieval sounding.

"Kevin, could you measure out the seeds for me? And, Ana, your job is to sift the flour."

Bella swiped her hand across her forehead, leaving a dusty smear of white flour above her eyebrow.

CREATURE FILE

SPECIES NAME: Bellanadae Superspyifus

KINGDOM: Anywhere! She can blend in like a chameleon if she wants, without anybody noticing her.

PHYLUM: Quiet Girls Who Are Secretly Incredibly Cool; New Best Friends Who Rock Short Hair

WEIGHT: She probably carries about fifty extra pounds worth of books with her everywhere.

HABITAT: The library, the art room, the museum. If it's somewhat geeky, she's into it (and that's awesome).

FEEDS ON: Books, cookies, and maps of exotic places.

LIFE SPAN: I bet if anyone could find the secret to immortality, it's Bella. It's got to be in a book somewhere, right?

HANDLING TECHNIQUE: None needed. Except when she's giving Daz a lovey-dovey look, in which case, I'm totally allowed to tell them they're gross. Because ew. How can anyone have a crush on my weirdo brother?!

I flipped through the recipe book in front of me, eyeing the cover suspiciously. A man with a bushy beard and beady eyes was holding a gold goblet. Bella's new cooking class had her "cooking through the ages," but I have to say, if these recipes were any indication, I would *not* want to live in the olden days. Any world without pizza doesn't seem like a world for me.

I used to think Bella was a lot like a mouse: super quiet and meek. That's how she seemed at school before I got to know her. But since Liv moved away and we became friends, now she seemed more like a hawk, with darting eyes that saw everything. I guess you can't know someone until you really talk to them. I'm just glad I *did*, so I didn't have to spend the entire summer surrounded by boys. Even if one of them is supercute.

"Are you sure about this?" I asked her. "I mean, *seed* bread? Won't that taste like birdseed?"

She shook her head and handed Daz a can of ginger ale. "It won't taste like birdseed because we're not *using* birdseed! We're using cardamom, coriander, anise, and other stuff. This recipe is supposed to be great, and my cooking instructor said that people have been making it for centuries! It's going to be perfect for the bake sale at the old-age home, but I have to test everything first. I want to do a bread, those no-bake cookies that you tried earlier, and something else *unique*," she said, excitement glittering in her eyes.

"I read that bread dates back to over twenty-two thousand five hundred years ago," Kevin said. "Some cultures even added rice, lentils, or peas to it."

I blinked at him. Sometimes I think Kevin should be a teacher because he's awesome at remembering facts and making things interesting for everyone. But honestly, *pea* bread? That would taste royally disgusting with peanut butter, I bet.

"Wait, we have to put *pop* in it?!" Daz squinted suspiciously as he read from the recipe book.

Bella sighed. "We only need to use a third of a cup for the recipe, but it has to be warm, so put it in the microwave for thirty seconds."

She gave me a look that I see on my mom a lot

when Daz is acting like a weirdo. I still couldn't believe that Bella saw *anything* in my completely insane brother, but ever since we all went to the end of school dance together as a group, she'd been pretty googly-eyed over him. And worse? *He* was all googly-eyed over her too! Well, most people wouldn't notice I bet because he's still a nutcase, but I definitely can see how he tries to make his hair extra spiky when Bella's around. My brother, the world's biggest clown, falling for the quietest girl I've ever met. Love is so weird.

Ew. I can't believe I just used that word to describe my brother. Barf.

Bella raised her voice. "That's your job. Daz! Are you paying attention?"

"Okay, okay," Daz huffed. He snapped open the can and dutifully measured out the ginger ale for the microwave while I sifted the white and wheat flour.

"So…" I said tentatively. "I have a bit of a problem." I handed my bowl to Bella, who reached across to give it to Kevin. My heart blippity-blipped when I saw the perfect little piles of measured spices on his cutting board. Honestly, he's even adorable helping out in the kitchen, so neat and organized. Unlike Daz, who had already spilled the pop over the counter and mopped it up with the sleeve of his shirt.

"What's up?" Bella stirred her bowl of butter and

sugar, creaming them together in a gooey paste. I reached over to sneak a taste. I'd been waiting for this moment ever since Ashley left the zoo yesterday, pretending she was practically best friends with Patricia. *Now* I could tell my friends and get a real game plan down.

"Well. I started at the new shark exhibit, right? And everyone was saying that because of my presentation, there's been a lot of people from local schools that want to volunteer there now too." Already I could feel the heat grow in my face. And not happy-watching-Kevin heat. Angry-trembly-earthquake-in-my-heart heat.

"And I got assigned to work with a new student."

"And what's the problem?" Bella asked.

I took a deep breath. "It's Ashley."

There. That should get their attention.

Bella's eyebrows knit together. "*Ashley* Ashley? Ashley, the one you call *Sneerer*, Ashley?" she asked. She set down her spoon, but that wasn't nearly the reaction I was hoping for. At least she could look mortified on my behalf. Even Kevin was frowning at his shoes. Like I'd told him a bad weather report, instead of announcing my own personal Anapocalypse.

"Hey!" I said. "*I* don't call her that!" I sat taller. "I mean, I do, but only because she calls me names right back. But you're not focusing on the problem. The problem is she's trying to ruin my life!"

Kevin cleared his throat. "Uh…" he started.

Finally, someone who *gets it*.

"But how could she do that?" he asked. "I mean, you're in the zoo, surrounded by a bunch of people, and she's not going to want to risk anything like her own reputation to make you look bad, right?" He blinked.

Honestly boys can be so dumb sometimes. Even the genius ones.

"That's *exactly* what she would do, Kev. I don't know *how* she would do it. I just know that she is *going* to!" I snapped. I looked to Bella for her to agree. But she was still looking at me like she was confused. "Right?" I lifted my eyebrows, giving her the "help-me-out-here" look.

She pursed her lips. I could tell she was doing that thing she always does, where she weighs what she wants to say in her head before she says it.

"I don't know. I think that maybe this whole thing with you and Ashley got way out of hand, and maybe she needed to volunteer somewhere during the summer like everyone else. It's possible that she just wants to get on with her life." She looked at Daz. "You know?"

"You're out of your mind!" I said. Instantly,

shame overcame me as I dropped my eyes to my hands. "I'm sorry," I said. "I don't see how you guys can be so chill about this. This is the girl that has tried to make my life a living you-know-what for like a billion years? And now she shows up in, like, the stinkiest, least Sneerer place on earth, and you act like it's no big deal?" I sputtered. "She is *obviously* going to try to sabotage me!"

"You can't let someone mess with you just because you're paranoid, Ana," Kevin said softly.

I stared at him. "Paranoid?! It's not paranoid if someone is actually out to get you!"

"Okay," Bella said. "Did she actually do anything yesterday?"

I nodded fast. "Yes! She was super nice to Patricia and acted like we were old friends. She even actually *tried* when we had to learn about shark species together, and made notes and everything," I said, jabbing my finger into a pile of flour.

Kevin frowned. "That doesn't sound bad." He looked to Bella for her reaction, but she shook her head. "Is it possible you're overreacting?"

Overreacting. *Honestly.*

"It sounds to me like she was trying to be nice, Ana," she said.

"But don't you get it?" I shouted. "Ashley being

nice is her trick! She's trying to convince everybody she's super nice so she can ruin me forever!"

Stupid Ashley, I seethed. If nothing had changed, then I wouldn't be sitting here talking about her and this stupid stuff.

Why did Bella have to be so...understanding?! And Kevin? He was supposed to *like* me maybe, so why was he not saying he wanted to come up with some super-genius plan to get Ashley kicked out of the zoo or something?

"You know, everyone has their own battles," Kevin mumbled. "I think Plato said that," he added with a sheepish grin. "I don't think you should worry because Ashley is probably trying to do her own thing, and for some reason, she has to be at the zoo, you know?"

I stared, dumbfounded. "You're talking about a dead guy at a time like this?" I shook my head. My friends, the people who were supposed to care most about me, were telling me not to worry about Ashley. Doesn't that sound *wrong*? That's like saying, "Oh, that's just a river full of piranhas. Why don't you hop in?" Or, "Hey, I've got some expired milk here. Let's have a smoothie!"

But I wasn't getting anywhere with them.

I slumped back on my chair and took a bite of the cookies Bella had made earlier. "Okay," I mumbled through my chewy mouthful. "I'll wait and see how it goes. You're right." I could feel the frustration bubbling inside me, but I shoved it down further with more cookies.

Daz narrowed his eyes at me and started to open his mouth, but I shoved a cookie at him before he could talk. There was no point trying, especially when they didn't see Ashley yesterday.

I needed a plan.

And this time, I knew what to do.

At home that night, I marched to my room. I was a girl on a mission, and there was no *way* Ashley was going to ruin my summer. If she was going to invade my life, then I was going to adapt and be *ready* for it this time. *Carpe sneerum* and all that.

"I'm not going to miss anything," I said, narrowing my eyes at Darwin. Earlier in the summer, Mom had given me a stack of empty blue notebooks that she'd gotten from her office. I dug around my desk drawer and pulled one out along with a big black marker.

Now I had a use for it.

I wrote in big, block letters.

THE OFFICIAL ANTI-ASHLEY NOTEBOOK

This is the official anti-Ashley book. I hereby swear that I, Ana Wright, will document all suspicious encounters with Ashley in this book. That way, when she ultimately tries to sabotage me (which is clearly inevitable), there will be a record of it all, and Bella and Kevin can see that no matter how much they wanted to BELIEVE in Ashley being GOOD, it just wasn't true.

I tapped my chin with my pen as I thought some more. Then I scribbled a messy list on the next page.

Ana's Super-Sneaky List of Ways to Avoid Ashley's Sabotage

1. Install a video camera in all areas where she and I will be working. Pro: This would guarantee I don't miss a thing. Con: Too darn expensive.

2. Hire someone to follow both of us around, watching her every move. This will ensure there is proof when Ashley decides to show her evil self. Pro: Having a super-duper bodyguard would probably come in handy when I needed to grab things from the top shelf of the cupboard too. Con: Also expensive. Why can't my parents give me a bigger allowance? I barely had enough

money for a banana split a week. Clearly a girl needs more than ONE of those a week, right?

3. Train a hawk to watch over me. I read somewhere that people used to use birds all the time to help them hunt. Maybe I could train one to follow me? Pirates have parrots. Why wouldn't I have a hawk? Pro: A hawk fairy godmother would probably be easy to hide, as it could fly away whenever someone wondered why a bird was following me. Con: I'd have to keep dead mice in my pocket to feed it, and there's no way I'm doing that again. There is nothing worse than finding a crusty mouse carcass in your pants. Gross.

I slammed the cover shut, feeling empowered. Ashley probably had her *own* book, called *How to Ruin Ana's Life*. Before heading downstairs for dinner, I hid the book in my backpack's secret compartment. The weight on my shoulders lightened a teensy bit, knowing I had a real plan.

Bring it, summer.

Chapter 6

The lionfish has up to eighteen needle-like spikes that carry venom. A sting from a lionfish can cause nausea and breathing difficulties.

—*Animal Wisdom*

The more I hear about these sea creatures, the more I'm so jazzed up to get in the water! Can you smell my sarcasm or what? Is it too much to ask for something cuddly every once in a while?!

I took a huge breath and dipped my head under the water again, with panic hitting me like an ice-cold wall.

I can do this. I'm not going to drown. Nope. Except it's really hard to do those deep, cleansing breaths underwater.

In. I tried to suck in a breath.

Out. The ragged *whoosh* of air was loud in my ears, fake and rattling.

A trail of goose bumps snaked up the back of my neck as I clenched the snorkel tighter in my mouth, feeling closer to gagging by the second.

When I tried to suck in another breath, the mask on my face stopped me from getting any air. I couldn't breathe.

I couldn't breathe!

"Don't breathe through your nose!" Patricia bellowed as I lurched my head up from the tank. Ashley slapped me on the back as I choked, hacking up a mouthful of cold, stinging water. My hair was stuck against my face like sloppy, wet tentacles. I was officially a sea monster.

Could Patricia have given Ashley and me something fun or *easy* for our first day together?

Of course.

But did she? Big nope.

Instead, she decided we should practice our snorkeling skills on the edge of the shark tank by dunking our faces underwater like we were bobbing for apples.

According to her, it *should* be easy to breathe through a straw, but I was pretty sure this was a form of torture somewhere.

"I can't get it!" I wailed. "Why is this so *hard*?!" I yanked the mask from my face and squished my cheeks. The rubbery suction had left indents on my skin that hurt to touch. Ashley gave me a sympathetic look, but I wasn't letting her fool me with that. I'd spent all morning preparing for the worst of Ashley's insults, like a warrior arming herself for her first day of battle.

But the weird thing was, Ashley hadn't done anything yet. She'd shown up on time, put her bag in her locker (which was right beside mine), and asked me how my morning was.

Clearly she was up to something.

"It's not hard." Ashley giggled. "It's just *breathing*! You do it all the time! In! Out! Repeat!"

I watched as Ashley stuffed the snorkel into her mouth and leaned over the edge of the pool, gracefully dipping her head under the water again. Her painted yellow fingernails glittered as she pointed dramatically to the top of her snorkel as she loudly breathed in and out.

"Show off," I muttered. It didn't surprise me that Ashley was good at snorkeling. I bet she snorkeled all the time, and suntanned on the beach, and sashayed across the sand to harp music or something. Ashley was probably good at everything. I watched her arch her neck and turn her head before coming up from the water again, forcing her wet hair to fall in one smooth sheet across her shoulder. A sudden thought popped into my head. *I bet Ashley has kissed a boy.*

She removed her mask and shifted the snorkel away from her mouth. For a moment, I wished that there was some obvious signal that lit up whenever people had been kissed before. You know, like a red light flashing above your head, so I could *know* who had been kissed and who hadn't. Then I realized that *I* would be wandering around *without* a light like a dimwit.

But.

I couldn't argue with the fact that practically every guy in our school (except Kevin, duh) gawks at Ashley whenever she walks down the hall, so it's not *unreasonable* to think that she's probably kissed a boy before. Maybe even more than one. What was her secret?

"All right, ladies, let's hit the shark tank." Patricia interrupted my thoughts. "Ana, if you don't want to snorkel in the tank, that's fine. But you'll probably find it easier to watch Ashley until you get the hang of it. You'll get there."

I rolled my eyes as she turned to point out the changing room.

"Follow me to get suited up, and we'll see how you do in some *real* water," she said. "All of the animals aren't in their tanks yet, but we thought it would be fun for you to try out the scuba suits." Patricia beamed. "We can't give you scuba tanks or anything, but we *did* manage to swing a few suits for the new aquarium and some snorkels. Some of the suits were junior sizes, so this is perfect! It will be a great experience."

Note: Whenever a grown-up says something is going to be a "great experience," you can pretty much guarantee it's going to be humiliating and/or suck.

"*Yaaay,*" I mumbled, following Ashley and Patricia into the back. I must have racked up some bad karma this year if I was spending my summer in yet *another* changing room with Ashley. Maybe I shouldn't have convinced Daz to eat that ancient Cheeto from under the couch last week.

Then I saw it.

Black rubber. Neon stripes. Lime-green flippers. *You've got to be kidding me.*

I stared at the scuba suit slung over the bench in front of me and exchanged glances with Ashley. Like it's every girl's dream to strip down in a changing room with the star of the swim team.

Here's the problem with scuba suits.

They are skintight.

That right there should explain it.

There's no hiding anything in them, especially that weird part of your butt that sometimes seems muffin-toppy, but you can never really be sure because there are no three-way mirrors in your house and there's no *way* you're asking someone to check.

That meant my entire body was going to be stuck in a rubbery black casing like some sort of weirdo sausage with electric-blue and neon-yellow darts. I backed away slightly, with my breakfast going flippity-flop inside my stomach. Could I sneak out and go hang out with my crocodiles instead?

You know things are bad when you catch me wanting to wear a safari hat.

"Think maybe we could test the waters...without the suit?" I asked Patricia, who was riffling through her own locker for her lunch. "I mean, not *naked*, obviously. But maybe in swimsuits?" I sputtered. *Or fully clothed even?*

"I don't see what the big deal is." Ashley sniffed. "I used one every day when my parents took me to Saint Barts. I think this is a *great* idea, Ms. Shurman." She batted her eyes at Patricia.

Ms. Shurman. Honestly.

I made a mental note to add that to my Anti-Ashley notebook. *Sarcastic and two-faced. Who the heck names a place Saint Barts anyway?*

But Patricia fell for it, instantly breaking into a smile. "Thank you, Ashley! I was so glad to see on your application that you were on the swim team at school," she gushed. "It will be a great help here. It will be a change for you to be near water with animals in it!"

My arms dropped to my sides. *I* could swim too. Not everyone needed those stupid medals to prove that.

Patricia kept talking. "Why don't I let you help Ana with hers and I'll meet you out by the tanks in a few minutes?" she said. "I have to meet our new co-op student. He should be here any minute."

I mumbled to myself as Patricia bustled out of the room. The fluorescent lights above us flickered, and it already smelled like salty seawater. But this was no day at the beach.

"You're sure you didn't have anything better to do today?" I asked Ashley. My throat felt tight. "Like maybe be anywhere but here?" I knew it was mean, but I wasn't about to let her even get a head start on me.

Her lips curled up. "You should be thankful I am, or else you'd have no idea how to fit into this." She held up her scuba suit, letting the legs flop against her leg. "If you can fit at *all*, that is."

"I don't need your help," I said firmly, squishing

my lips together. I tried to keep my eyes down and focus on my scuba suit, figuring out what part of me went where first. Did you step into it like onesie pajamas? Or back into it like a beeping truck into a parking lot? I tugged at the zipper on the chest.

It didn't budge.

"You're sure you don't want some help?" Ashley cooed, shooting me a teasing glance. She had unzipped hers already and was staring at me with her hand on her hip and an amused look on her face. How could she be so comfortable with this? I imagined that red light flashing above her head again.

Not only can I put on a scuba suit, but I've definitely kissed a boy. If it were me, I'd have this kissing pact thing done by dinnertime. She didn't have to say the words out loud. They were screaming inside my own head.

Maybe help from Ashley wasn't the *worst* thing I could get. *Maybe* if I were nice to her, some of that sparkly Ashley mojo would rub off on me. Was it worth it?

I dropped the scuba suit back on the chair and squared my shoulders.

"Okay, fine," I said, already feeling about half an inch tall. "What do I do?"

She crossed her arms and stepped closer. "You wearing your swimsuit under that mess you've got on?" She raised her eyebrows. I looked down at my outfit. Khaki zoo shorts and a red tank top. I thought I looked okay. At least I did until she walked in with her hair perfectly curled at the ends like that.

"Yes," I hissed. Not that I was going to show her.

"Well, this goes on over the top of your swim-suit," she said. And with that, she tugged on the halter top of her dress and stepped out of it, showing off a perfect neon-green bikini.

Seriously.

A bikini.

I practically choked on my own spit. "Um, you're wearing *that*?" I gawked at her. And yeah, okay. I admit it. I was jealous. Super jealous. Not of her little bikini (which I would never be caught DEAD in), but of her long legs and her chest that looks like those girls on the magazines at the checkout. Not that I was staring at her boobs. But it's kind of hard not to when they're right there staring *you* in the face. God, is it totally weird that I was looking at her boobs? I glared away angrily, focusing on my scuba suit. It was hanging there like a limp, aquatic scarecrow without a head.

She stood tall. "Why not? It's just an old swim-suit." She tucked a few pieces of hair behind her ear in the mirror before ducking over to the bench for the scuba suit.

"But you look…" I glared at her.

Like a swim team goddess.

Like a model.

Like a movie star.

"Ridiculous," I said, angrily tugging off my shirt. I had a navy blue one piece on under my clothes, and no matter how confident I pretended I was, stripping in front of Ashley was definitely not high on my list of Things That Make Ana Feel Peachy. At school, all the girls changed in the same room in gym class, but here there were no people to hide behind so the Sneerers couldn't get a look at me and my training-wheels chest.

She scoffed. "Step into each leg one at a time, and you have to sort of shimmy the fabric up your leg." She demonstrated, unraveling the suit over her tanned leg. "It's like putting on heavy pantyhose. Make sure the zipper is down and then yank it up over your hips when you're done."

I struggled with my suit, until it somehow got stuck around my waist. I was officially a scuba sausage.

"Argh!" I said, turning my back to Ashley while I tried to rearrange the slippery fabric over my hip. I was *not* going to ask for her help again. I was not.

"Here, let me," Ashley said.

"No."

"You sure? Mine's on okay." She stood with her hip jutted out. Even in the stupid scuba suit, she looked like she could be on some vacation magazine for the tropics. Or a dolphin-saving superhero with fantastic hair.

"Of course it is," I mumbled.

"Patricia's going to be waiting." She sighed. "Just let me help you. You don't need to be such a priss."

"What do you care about her waiting?" I glared at her but let my arms drop when she came over to me and started jimmying the suit. So much for not letting Ashley get the upper hand—now here she was zipping me up like a four-year-old in a snowsuit.

Now I was a humiliated scuba sausage.

"Okay, okay," I said, pulling away from her when the suit was on properly.

She glared at me. "You're *welcome*."

"Thanks," I muttered.

I was about to say something to regain my dignity when we stepped out of the changing room, but Ashley stopped short as soon as the door was open. I slammed into her back.

"Hey, what the—" I said.

"Oh. My. God." Ashley's voice was a hushed whisper. "*Ana*." She reached behind her, aimlessly clutching at my arm.

I thought maybe one of the sharks had been brought in and that Ashley was freaked out. At least, that's what I hoped. Then she would run away from the zoo in her perfect little scuba suit and never come back.

But then I saw it.

Or rather, I saw *him*.

When we were younger, my parents took us to see the Grand Canyon. It was awesome and epic, and the moment we walked up to the edge of the viewing platform, my heart seemed to stop. I couldn't speak, and my eyes felt like they were going to dry out because I never wanted to blink again. Mom said it was normal to stare in wonder when you saw something magnificent. Something that made you realize how amazing this whole big universe can be.

Well, the Grand Canyon has nothing on the six-foot-four-inch sandy-haired god standing in front of us.

"Girls, this is Logan," Patricia introduced us. "He's a marine biology student, and he'll be helping us out this summer."

CREATURE FILE

SPECIES NAME: Logan Adonis

KINGDOM: *My heart!*

PHYLUM: Guys Who Look Like They Could Be Underwear Models on the Side of a Bus Somewhere, But Instead They're Here in Front of You and Oh My God How Do I Breathe Again?

WEIGHT: Too busy drooling to care.

FEEDS ON: I mean seriously, *look at him!* I could swim *laps* in those eyes!

LIFE SPAN: Whatever it is, it isn't long enough.

HANDLING TECHNIQUE: I...I think I forgot how to sentence.

Ashley sucked in her cheeks, giving her best smile. She didn't seem to mind the fact that she was in a goofy suit. "Hi, Logan! I'm Ashley! I'm a summer student too!"

His face lit up, and I had to stop myself from staggering backward. He was even more gorgeous when he smiled. The sides of his eyes went up like his whole face was happy. If he could bottle that, nobody on earth would ever be sad again.

"Hey, ladies. Nice to meet ya." He reached out and shook our hands. The smell of woodsy cologne and sunshine wafted over me. How can someone smell like actual *sunshine*?

I was never washing my hand again.

Patricia smirked the tiniest bit. "Logan is from California, where he's studying marine biology in college, specifically sharks." Logan nodded proudly, sending his golden hair over his eyes. He combed it back casually with his fingertips.

Nngggghhh.

"Ooh, I love sharks!" Ashley blurted.

What? Are you kidding me?

"Me too," Logan said. His voice reminded me of rich, dark chocolate. I don't even like dark chocolate, but it was enough to make me a total convert. Is this what twentyish-year-old guys were like? Is this what *Kevin* would be like when he was Logan's age? With a deep voice and tiny lines around his mouth and gold hair on his arms?

The thought made my insides blush. I *know* that insides can't technically blush, but this was a special circumstance, I guess. It was like he walked off a movie set!

Instantly, I didn't want to be me. I wanted to be Ana*stasia*, not plain old Ana. I wanted to look like I walked off some teen movie set too. Then Kevin would *definitely* kiss me.

Oh God, he was talking. *Pay attention!*

"I normally spend summers with my uncle on the water, but the opportunity here was too good to pass up. This new exhibit should be wild." He looked up around us, clearly impressed. I would have agreed if he'd said Daz's ratty sneakers were impressive, but hey.

"Ana's grandfather is actually the one funding it," Patricia explained.

"Oh right!" Logan exclaimed. "You're Shep Foster's grandkid! I forgot!"

I smiled tightly. I wasn't exactly thrilled with the idea of him thinking of me as some little girl, especially not someone's grandkid. It made me sound so *young*. But he was still staring at me with those sparkly blue eyes…

"Yeah, he's my mom's dad," I said awkwardly. Like he didn't know what the concept of "grandfather" meant. Good one, Ana. My heart was doing hopscotch in my chest.

He grinned at me easily. "Shep's awesome. I saw that special on TV where he got bit by that snake… man." He shook his head. "I'd love to meet him in person sometime."

"Ana's family is all kinds of crazy like that," Ashley blurted. There was more than a hint of buzzing excitement in her eyes.

I concentrated hard.

Must. Make. Words. Happen.

"He's back in LA right now, but he'll be here for sure when the exhibit opens," I said. "I can introduce you if you want." Pretty sure I've never been happier about getting a single sentence out of my mouth without garbling it up.

"That'd be great!" A loud guitar riff startled me. "Sorry, that's my phone." He held up his hand and dug around in his pocket. "I have to take this, but it was awesome meeting you. Should be fun seeing you guys around!" Ashley waved coyly as he took his phone call, wandering off into the sunset, er...I mean, down the hallway. Something about Logan demanded an epic exit.

"Whoa," Ashley said. "That guy is a certified hottie."

I stood there, watching the space where Logan had been standing.

"Yeah," I breathed.

"Did...did he say we'll get to work with him?" Ashley turned to me. She looked as dazed as I probably did. "Is that what he just said?" She leaned back against the wall, like she couldn't trust her legs to hold her up.

I tried to remember. "Yes. Yes, he did."

Ashley turned expectantly to Patricia, with a look of "don't-leave-me-hanging-here." Patricia sighed. "Yes, girls. He will be helping out around here and doing some work on his thesis. You're welcome." She rhymed the words off in a monotone voice.

My face went hot. A whole month of the Sun

God. This must have been prophesized in some ancient book.

Patricia clapped her hands. "All right! Don't make me get out the hose to cool you down. Have we had enough of the hormones for today then?" She rolled her eyes. "I won't have you ogling the scenery here on my time, *thankyouverymuch*. There's no point in wasting those suits. Go ahead and see what it's like!"

Ashley and I waddled to the tank, with our lime-green flippers smacking the floor like duck feet. It doesn't get more glamorous than this, does it?

Chapter 7

The mantis shrimp is able to strike out its claws with the same velocity as a gunshot from a twenty-two caliber rifle.

—*Animal Wisdom*

yikes?!

The sound of frantic footsteps and tinkling water filled my ears. A few days (and many annoying snorkel sessions) later, it finally happened: Shark Day was here. The new exhibits were full, and there were dozens of new creatures for us to meet before the exhibit officially opened to the public in a grand opening two weeks from now.

And of course, Grandpa wanted it to be a big surprise.

"Everyone keep your eyes closed!" he said, beaming with excitement.

Mom, Dad, Daz, Sugar, Ashley, and I stood with our eyes scrunched shut, waiting for Grandpa's go-ahead to open them.

Sugar gripped my hand tightly. "Ooh, I am so excited, Ana doll! It even *sounds* beautiful!"

"Ready, Patricia?" Grandpa said.

I tried to peek through my eyelashes, but all I could see were his feet.

"Yep! Ladies and gentlemen. One, two, three, *OPEN*!"

"Whoa," I breathed, gaping at the room in awe. Mom and Ashley stumbled back, taking in the room, while Sugar's eyes were bugging out in shock. And naturally, Daz began completely wigging out.

"Grandpa, this is *so cool*!" he squeaked.

It *was* cool. The empty horseshoe-shaped tank had been filled with a beautiful mangrove forest, with roots, rocks, and sandy areas jutting out around us. The water was pristine and clear, with viewing windows on each side.

And the best part?

Sharks! Tons of sharks swimming around us, all right there!

"Welcome to the mangrove forest," Grandpa said softly. His eyes shone with pride. "The center exhibit is all animals that kids can touch." He pointed to a group of rays with broad fins sailing past us in the water. "Cownose rays and Atlantic rays." Ducking over to a thicket of roots, he said, "Epaulette sharks over here."

Patricia beamed at him. "And over here"—she pointed to a small, round tank on the floor—"is the tide pool."

Daz leaned over the water, while Ashley stuck closer to me. "Horseshoe crabs!" he exclaimed.

"Yep. And hermit crabs and starfish. Everything you'd want in your friendly neighborhood tide pool," Grandpa said. A lump caught in my throat as I saw him wipe a tear from his eye. It was easy to get caught up with how crazy he could be, but at times like this? It was seriously cool to have him as a grandpa.

"This is incredible," I said, letting my hand dip into the water below me. "For real. It's so awesome."

Ashley nodded, coming out of her dopey-eyed daze. "I can't believe it," she said. "It's like walking into a dream." She saw the surprised look on my face. "Only like a sciencey one, with lots of diagrams and stuff," she added, her ears turning pink.

"What are these?" I asked, walking over to the wall. The touch tanks were lined with side exhibits, ones that you couldn't touch, but they still bathed the room with an oceany-blue glow. A yellow crea-ture with leaflike lobes all over its body stared back at me.

"That's a leafy sea dragon," Mom said, touching her finger to the glass. "They were always one of my favorites." She wiped her eyes with her sleeve. "Thanks, Dad."

"Ooh! What's this over here?! Some sort of jel-lyfish? I like their little insides!" Sugar piped up. She scampered over to another tank, her high heels clicking on the floor.

"I've got this," Daz quipped, running over to her. He stuck out his chest. "Those are moon jellies. There are over two thousand different jellies in the world right now. And they don't have hearts! Or brains!"

Ashley snorted.

"What?" Daz said, giving his best innocent look. "I know about animals *too*, you know." He fake-whispered to Sugar, "Some girls don't know how to handle an intelligent man."

"Talk about brainless," I muttered to Ashley. She gave me a devilish grin.

"How do you live with him?" she whispered.

"You have *no* idea."

"So you guys want a quick lesson on how to inter-act with these guys or what?" Grandpa said. "You'll be the ones showing kids how to do it!"

"Yes!" Ashley blurted.

The five of us stood outside the largest tank, watching Grandpa and Patricia's example from the inner circle. The rays and sharks whisked by us, sending clear currents of water out in ripples around their tails. That's when it hit me. Did these things have teeth? I glanced down at my hand. I didn't want to lose any fingers here.

"The first rule is: be very quiet," Grandpa said. "They can hear you from under there, so if you have a bunch of kids in here that are being too loud, it's your job to keep them quiet so the animals don't get scared. If they do"—he pointed to a rocky shoal in the middle of the tank—"they will hide there."

Ashley's eyes were wide as she stared down at the fins that zipped by.

"Step two." He lifted his hand. "Let the sharks come to you. Not the other way around. These animals are very sensitive to touch, and chasing them will only spook them. You want to be gentle and put your hand palm side down under the water."

We all did as he said. The water was chilly, but I was more concerned by the creatures whooshing by me to notice. Daz was practically vibrating he was so excited. I'm surprised he hadn't just leaped in the tank yet and declared himself King Triton.

"And three," Patricia said. "When one does swim

under you, glide your hand along its back." She waited a moment for a ray to approach her, then stroked it lightly with her fingers as it went by.

It didn't even seem to mind!

I wanted to try. I concentrated hard, willing one of the rays to come close. After a few close calls, one finally swam right under my hand. I lowered my palm slightly, letting my fingertips drag gently on its back. A thrill ran through my body.

"That's so cool!" I said. "It feels like sandpapery skin!"

"I got one!" Daz announced. "It came right to me! I am the shark whisperer!"

Mom raised her eyebrows. "For a whisperer, you're awfully loud!"

Even Dad was getting in on the action, waiting patiently while a ray swished under his hand.

"They aren't coming to me," Ashley said. There was more than a note of sadness in her voice. I almost made a joke that sharks don't like Sneerers, but once I saw the defeated look on her face, I decided against it.

"Just keep your hands still." I helped her. "And your fingers straight out. They will come," I said. She held her breath as she listened, keeping her arm motionless under the water.

"Here he comes," I whispered, gripping her other arm.

Swoosh. Her fingers lowered slightly.

"I did it!" Ashley yelped. "It does feel like sandpaper! Only softer and spongy." She watched intently as the water dripped from her hand back into the tank.

As everyone was leaning over the water, I realized something. This was a definite *first* in my life. Yeah, it was the first time I'd ever touched sharks or rays. And the first time I got to touch a hermit crab. But as I watched closer, it was also the first time Ashley ever looked *happy.*

I mean, sure. She's happy in school, I guess.

Especially when I'd seen her talking to Zack or that guy who wears too much cologne. She always bats her eyelashes and giggles and smiles.

But that seemed different than now. The face she usually wore at school didn't look anything like the one she had when she was touching sharks. Could this be what Ashley *really* looked like when she was happy?

I let my thoughts swirl around in my head as I dipped my fingers in the water once more.

"Ana!" Sugar sidled up beside me. She was holding a hermit crab in her palm from the tidal pool tank. The red nail polish on her fingertips matched its orangey claws. "You've got to see his little feet. They are simply darlin'!"

Ashley bit her lip as she took a final look around the tanks. Her smile dropped.

"What's the matter, hun?" Sugar asked.

Blinking away the glassy look on her face, Ashley let out an overwhelmed sigh. "I always thought that these things were dangerous," she admitted, pointing to the touch tank. "I had no idea it was like this."

Mom nodded. "Many people think *all* sharks are vicious killers."

"The reality is, there are around four hundred and fifty species of sharks, and only a handful of them have ever tried to attack a human," Grandpa added. "These epaulette sharks eat crabs and shrimp. Most would rather stay far away from us in the wild."

Ashley nodded, and the rest of us were silent. Ashley looked shy now. Almost apologetic.

"I'm really glad we did this," I blurted, causing everyone to turn to me. "You know," I added, staring down at the water. "It's just really cool. I'm glad to be here."

Beside me, Ashley smiled. "Me too."

"That's great, girls. It sounds like you're going to learn a lot this summer!" Mom said airily.

I didn't miss the sly grin on her face.

Sometimes I think mothers are sneakier than they let on.

Chapter 8

The Japanese spider crab can grow to have a
leg span of thirteen feet.

—Animal Wisdom

why on earth does a crab need to be that big?
Is it planning on taking over the world?!

The next week went by swimmingly.

No pun intended.

With the animals in their tanks, Ashley and I
worked together for a couple hours every day. I didn't
even have any good material to add to my Anti-Ashley
notebook, no matter how hard I tried to think of
something. That notebook sat unused in my backpack, along with a tin of mints and my headphones.

Ashley had been so *not-sneery*, in fact, that I ended up giving one of my extra blue notebooks to her, so we could take notes about all the animals we'd have to learn about.

That's right.

Ana the Crocodile Girl had officially become a Shark Girl. Instead of presentations with reptiles, we were going to memorize short little snippets of information about the Adventure Zone creatures, so we could be there whenever kids had a question. With Grandpa organizing the big "grand opening" presentation for the public at the end of next week, we'd decided that since I'd already had my share of the spotlight, it was Ashley's turn to lead a presentation.

I won't lie.

It was sort of funny to see how nervous she was.

"How do you make sure you don't memorize the wrong facts for each animal?" she asked me on Friday, as she sat across from me at the zoo cafeteria. Piles of books on sharks and other sea creatures were stacked beside us. If I didn't know any better, I'd say it looked an awful lot like *school*.

Except school doesn't come with snow cones. I licked some of the sticky blue juice from the back of my hand and wiped up some of the drips from the open page of my notebook.

"You try to come up with little prompts to help you remember," I said. The truth was, I had no idea how I could remember random facts about animals. Probably because I've grown up with them, and my brain is a little off.

She frowned. "But...how?"

I opened one of the books, finding a page on cownose rays, one of the species in our tanks. "Like right here," I said, pointing to the page. I read aloud, "Cownose rays are known to travel in large groups of up to ten thousand." I put the book down.

"So you tell yourself, 'Cownose rays, schools of up to ten thousand,'" I explained. "And you remember it by thinking of a stampede of ten thousand *cows* charging through *school*. So the words *cow* and *school* and *ten thousand* should help you remember that one fact."

Ashley's eyes glazed over. "You do this for every animal you talk about?" She paused, flipping through the pages. "Is that what you did for your reptile presentation?"

I sat back in my chair. This was the first time either of us had mentioned that day. It brought a bitter taste to my mouth. "I knew most of those facts already," I admitted. "Because we've taken care of loads of reptiles at home. So it was easier for me to know what I was talking about then."

She nodded glumly, and something inside me stirred. Was it pity? It felt a lot like pity. Hot and clammy inside my chest. "It's not the same this time, though," I added. "There's a lot I don't know about with these guys." I tapped the books. "So I'm pretty much learning it for the first time too."

"Uh-huh," she said. She turned back to her notebook, where she had a list of the species inside the tank listed. There were lots of scribbled-out words marking up the page.

"I don't remember things easily," she said. "Not *lots* of things like this. It gets all jumbly in my head, like a puzzle with a zillion pieces."

I nodded. "Don't worry. If you need to use your notebook to help you, that's okay. Lots of people do, so make yourself some simple notes that are quick to read, and if you do any presenting, you can peek down quickly and see the facts you need, and then look back up to the crowd."

She took a deep breath. "The crowd. Right."

"Hey, girls!" Logan wove between the cafeteria tables to greet us. Ashley slid a napkin to me and gave me a pointed stare.

Grateful, I snatched it and wiped the snow cone juice from my lips before Logan could see.

"Hi!" Ashley cooed, settling back in her chair. "What are you doing here?"

You know, in school we learned that one of the smallest units of time was a nanosecond. But I think they were wrong. I think the smallest unit of time was the time it took for Ashley to go from looking sad to *totally and completely perky* again when Logan shows up. Meanwhile I was still stuck back ten seconds ago when we were talking about sharks.

"H-hey, Logan," I stammered. I glared at my books. I could tell from the heat in my cheeks you could probably fry an egg on my face.

He pulled up a chair beside us, stretching out his long legs under the table. It took every cell of my being not to start hyperventilating. *Why* was this guy so cute?! Was he some kind of android? How come every time I saw him I pictured *Kevin* as a twenty-year-old? And was it wrong that I wanted to smell him again?

Gah, stop being a psycho freak of nature!

"What are you guys up to?" he asked. He leaned forward to pick up a book, settling it open on his stomach. "Ahh, mantas! One of my favorites! I have a tattoo of a manta ray," he said deviously. "Wanna see it?"

"*Yes*," Ashley blurted.

I bit my lip to hold back my laugh. At least she'd said something, though. I was still staring at him like a fool.

He pulled up the sleeve on his work shirt to reveal a toned, tan forearm. "Check it," he said, flexing his hand. A silvery-blue manta ray wound its way around his arm, with a tail that ran up over his elbow.

"That is the coolest thing I've ever seen," Ashley said. Her eyes were practically bugging out of her head.

Not that I could blame her. It *was* super cool. Usually I don't like tattoos, but on Logan? He could have a tattoo of old cheese on him and it would look like fine art. I wonder if Kevin would ever get a tattoo? *Hmm.*

"Did it hurt?" Ashley asked.

He didn't have time to answer. "Hello? Anyone here?" A girl peeked her head into the room. "Oh! Logan, there you are!"

Ashley and I gawked as she ran over to him.

"Babe!" he exclaimed. He stood up and pulled her into a hug. Her feet even lifted off the ground!

Beside me, Ashley rolled her eyes. "Get a room," she whispered.

You'd expect that a total hottie like Logan would be dating another total hottie.

And you know what?

You'd be right.

She had long dark hair that was tied into a low ponytail and porcelain skin like a doll. I kid you not, she even smelled like strawberries. She was a walking stick insect in capri pants that smelled like a fruit basket.

I fidgeted with the spine of my notebook as they kissed. The kiss pact with Liv niggled away in my brain. Should I smell like strawberries? Would that get Kevin to kiss me?

"What are you doing here? I thought you weren't supposed to get here until tonight?" Logan asked, when they pulled themselves apart. Took them long enough.

"Early flight!" she exclaimed. "I thought I'd do some poking around here today! I've been looking for you for *ages*," she said, her eyes sweeping the area before settling on us. Was it just me or did she look sort of nervous?

"Guys, this is Danielle," Logan said.

Ashley's eyebrow arched. "Hey. I'm Ashley," she said. I watched with amazement. She didn't seem fazed at *all*. Meanwhile I was basically tripping over my tongue, thinking about how these two had been playing tonsil hockey five seconds ago.

"Ana," I said when she turned to me. There. I could talk again.

"Wait," she said. "Ana Wright?" Whipping a notepad from her purse, she rushed toward me.

I edged away. "Um, yeah?" I said.

"Would you mind if I asked you a couple questions?" she asked. "I would *love* to get a statement from you for my college newspaper! I'm writing a piece about your grandfather!" She tapped her foot. I got the distinct feeling that hanging around this girl for more than five minutes would give me a twitch. She was *intense*. Her eyes bored a hole in my head.

"A statement?" I croaked.

"You know," she said, waving her hands dismissively. "Shep Foster's very own granddaughter working at the zoo! I'd love your opinion on the exhibits and the work you're doing here."

"Okay, sure," I said.

"Can you take me through some of the daily tasks here?" she asked, holding her pen stiffly above her notepad.

I sat straighter. "The student ambassadors just try to help out with background stuff," I said. "We help prepare food, or clean, or do some super-small presentations with kids. It's all volunteer work, and it goes toward school credit each year." I wanted to make it sound glamorous, but let's face it, cleaning poop and fish heads wasn't exactly a red carpet walk. "Ashley and I are helping in the new marine exhibit."

She nodded. She hadn't written anything down yet.

"Shep is like the most exciting person *ever*," she said, blinking fast. "Does anything crazy happen here? The drama must follow him everywhere." Her words felt like tiny arrows piercing me, fast and sharp.

"He's exciting, all right," I said. I tried not to roll my eyes. "But generally things around here are pretty… normal. For a zoo, I mean. All the zookeepers make sure that everything stays on schedule and safe." I rambled off our zoo director Paul's usual speech. It was one of the first I'd learned when I started to hang out here.

"Is he going to be around for the first presentation in the new Adventure Zone?" Her voice was light, but there was a hard look in her eyes. She reminded me of those journalists that showed up when I did my presentation in June, always starting sentences and waiting for me to finish them. And maybe mess up. If there was one thing I knew from Grandpa, it was that newspapers *loved* when people said the wrong thing or caused a big uproar.

"Dani, baby," Logan said, pulling her under his arm. "Ana probably doesn't want to deal with your questions right now," he said.

He leaned closer to me to fake-whisper. "Dani's a journalism student *and* an animal nut," he said with a knowing nod. "She's been so excited about coming here she hasn't shut up about it in weeks. Meeting Shep Foster and his famous granddaughter." He waved his hands in the air and gave me a wink.

Oh, my heart. Logan seriously had to stop winking at me like that if I was expected to use proper words.

"Oh, shush," Danielle said. Her face flushed, giving her cheeks a peachy glow. Not that I could blame her. If Logan had his arm around *me*, I'd probably be a puddle on the floor right now. I didn't know how that girl was even staying upright with those eyes staring at her.

Maybe *she's* the android.

"We'll leave you guys to your notes," Logan said.

The two of them walked away, locked in some sort of love-octopus hug. It seemed like they had more than two arms each. Did getting a boyfriend suddenly mean you sprouted an extra arm for all that hand-holding and hugging? I wondered for a moment how Danielle seemed so *not* nervous kissing Logan, but when I thought about kissing Kevin, I could barely think straight.

"I don't like her," Ashley said when the door shut behind them.

I scoffed. "Of course you don't. She gets to kiss Logan."

"It's not only that," she said. "She gives me the creeps. She's one of those girls who is super nice to your face, but I bet she's a real jerk."

I stared at her, surprised. "What? Are *you* actually

talking about people being mean?" I couldn't believe what I was hearing.

Ashley glared. "Forget it," she said.

The chill from her words made me shiver.

She shook her head. "I'm just saying. I don't like her."

"Yeah, well." I sighed heavily. "Luckily you don't have to hang out with her. It's not like you had a chance with Logan in the first place. He's like twenty years old."

Ashley looked unimpressed. "Whatever. In ten years he'll be thirty and I'll be twenty-three. That's not that big of a difference."

I scrunched my nose. "Yes, it is! He'd never go out with you!"

Ashley's frown began to twitch. "Okay, fine. In fifteen years then. I'll be"—she counted in her head—"twenty-eight. And he will be thirty-five."

"You know that means he'll almost be our *parents'* age then, right?" I loved bursting her little bubble.

"Ahh! Why do you always have to ruin everything?!" She shoved me on the shoulder, but for a moment I could see the glimmer of something else in her eye. And it wasn't hate this time.

It was Ashley joking around.

It was totally creepy, but almost...*nice*.

"Hey," she said suddenly. "Did you figure out

what you're going to wear for opening day? I want to get a new top for the presentation."

"I don't know." I hung my head. I had tried to figure out how to get a better swimsuit for under my zoo uniform without having to actually *shop* for one. Training bras were one thing, but swimsuits? That was a whole new level of awkward. "Everything I have at home doesn't fit anymore," I admitted.

"I can help you, you know," Ashley said. She blinked at me expectantly.

"What do you mean? Help me with an outfit?" I couldn't stop my voice from squeaking like a mouse.

"Obviously."

"I think I'm good," I said. I had no idea what she had in mind, but Ashley's help wasn't something I was eager to beg for. Although she did have great style. But still. Had to be a trap. This wasn't hanging out at the zoo together. Shopping would mean the mall. *Her* territory. At least here I was surrounded by sharks and crocodiles and other creatures that could keep me safe. Once I learned to control them like an army, that is.

Ugh, I'm turning into Daz.

"Oh, come on," she said, glaring at me. "Let me help already. We can go shopping at the mall and get new suits. I haven't gone shopping in weeks," she whined.

I stiffened. This had to be some sort of joke. Some evil plot to get me in a dressing room so she could grab all my clothes and leave me in the dust, wandering naked through the mall. Can you imagine *that* headline?

"Shopping?" I asked. "Together?"

She shrugged. "Why not?"

Now it was my turn to give her a look. Because you've hated me since first grade. Because you make my life a living hell. Because you volunteered to work in the zoo simply because you enjoy *torturing* me.

But I didn't say any of that.

Because I wasn't *sure* of any of it. At least, the last bit.

"Oh come on, Ana," she said. "I know we've been jerks to each other, but maybe we can just…drop it for the summer. You know?"

Jerks to each *other*? Since when was I jerky to *her*?

She clucked her tongue when she saw the question in my eyes. "There's no reason why we can't help each other out."

There was the catch.

"What do you need help with?"

She batted her best doe eyes. But underneath, her face was hard, like she was trying to look strong. "I'm nervous for the presentation," she said finally. "I just want a chance to practice for someone, and Patricia is too busy, and my sister is always at the gym for swim trials." She shrugged. "And you're here."

I hesitated.

"And you already know what I have to say, so you can actually be *helpful*. You know?" She tapped her foot. "We can make those memorization notes together for me to use."

The walls began to feel tight around me. I guess it *sort of* made sense for us to help each other out. Or did it? I tried to imagine telling Bella or Liv about going shopping with Ashley. That would be like telling them I'd suddenly taken up Latin for the fun of it. Since when did being almost thirteen come with so many tough decisions? But Ashley wasn't acting like any of this was tough. She was confident and acting like this was no big deal.

But was that part of her trick?

"I'll have to think about it," I said. I hated myself for being so wishy-washy. I wanted to *know* for sure what I wanted to do, instead of feeling like one giant question mark. But this felt too weird to be true.

Ashley nodded. "'Kay, give me a call tonight if you want to go. We can meet tomorrow afternoon. That will give us almost a week to get our outfits ready for next *Saturdayyyy*," she said in a singsong voice. Reaching into her purse, she pulled out a teeny pink notecard with a kitten on it, with her telephone number written in calligraphy. See what I mean? Ashley had a *card* like a businesswoman.

I took it from her and stuffed it into my pocket. "All right. I'll let you know." I gathered my books and left as quickly as I could without looking like a total freak.

I had some thinking to do.

Chapter 9

Giant cuttlefish have green blood.

—Animal Wisdom

So cuttlefish are like the Incredible Hulks of
the sea then?

In the safety of my own room, nestled next to the
hippos and away from Ashley's eagle eyes, I pulled
out my Anti-Ashley notebook. *Technically*, her
asking me to go shopping wasn't a mean thing. But
it was *about* her, so I still counted it as an Ashleyism
for the notebook.

"Okay, Darwin," I said, poking him in his feathery shoulder with the pen cap. "You need to help
me here."

He stared at me with his dark, beady eyes and scratched at his cheek lazily with one long claw. Darwin was always a bit of a slacker when you needed help. Not like the *real* Darwin, I bet. He looks super helpful in a nice-old-man kind of way.

I started a new page and wrote in my big, bubble letters.

To Go or Not to Go: The Pros and Cons of Shopping with Ashley

"Well?" I tapped my pen against my chin. "Let's hear it. Something *good* about shopping with Ashley."

Darwin blinked.

"Useless bird," I mumbled. "Okay. How about this?" I started to write.

Pro: I desperately need a new swimsuit. My navy blue one is too small, and it rides up my butt and digs into my shoulders like nobody's business. The last thing I need is someone snapping a picture of me in that monstrosity and plastering my wedgie in all its glory over the Internet.

I frowned to myself, as Darwin skittered around my desk and bobbed in front of my mirror. He ducked his head, preening his shoulder with his beak and cooing at his own reflection. What a complete diva.

"You're right," I said. "She's totally vain. So she'd probably make shopping all about her, and I'd be stuck watching her do her runway walk in great outfits the whole time without actually getting any help." I wrote that in the cons list.

"But on the other hand," I said, my hand poised over the paper. "If she *does* help me, the fact that she's vain could be a good thing. I could use someone who actually knows *how* to look good and buy the right clothes, you know? She always looks awesome, and it would be a huge pro if she could help me look even remotely hot."

Darwin didn't look convinced.

"Trust me," I added, filling in more of the pros column. "It is crazy hard to look good in a swimsuit. I need all the help I can get."

Darwin whistled and gawked at me. Clearly he agreed.

"But!" I shouted suddenly, startling him. "The whole thing could be a trap!" I scribbled some more, rambling. "I mean, if she wanted to go shopping, why wouldn't she go with Rayna or Brooke, or even her mom? Why would she ask me? That probably means it's definitely a trap and her *only* goal here is to get me in some awful position with some super-sketchy swimsuit of horror so she can post it online for the whole world to see."

I puckered my lips in contemplation. Darwin cocked his head, bobbing excitedly. He started making shrill kissy noises, peppered with the flirty whistles.

"Ugh, that's right." I agreed. The realization hit me like a rhino stampede. "The kiss pact." I wrote in the pros column. "Getting Ashley's help with looking good would definitely help out with Kevin. I don't have much time left!" I glanced to my desk calendar. The summer had practically just started, but it felt like school would be here faster than Daz could eat a bag of Cheetos. Time was already running out.

I *had* to get Kevin to kiss me. There was no way Liv would *ever* let me hear the end of it if I failed. And as much as I hated to admit it, Ashley was pretty much the only girl I knew (who wasn't, like, my mom) that I could ask for help with kissing tips.

"I'm pretty sure that counts as more than one pro," I explained, underlining it a few times.

Staring at my list, I knew what I had to do.

Already I felt like I was going to throw up. The last time I'd felt so nervous about something was right before I did my big crocodile presentation when school ended. I had *really* wanted to see if I could do it, but part of me felt too paralyzed to move.

This was exactly the same, only instead of wanting to present in front of people, I wanted to see if I was brave enough to face Ashley, who was even *scarier* than crocodiles.

I looked past my computer at the photo on my desk that Grandpa had given me from my presentation. My own face stared back at me, beaming with pride in front of the big crowd of people.

I had been so scared, just a few minutes earlier. Would facing a shopping trip with Ashley turn out the same way? Maybe something good *could* come from it?

There was only one way to find out.

I picked up my phone and dug out the pink card from my pocket. The tiny kitten face stared back at me, daring me to chicken out. *You're not afraid of a teensy kitten, are you?* it seemed to say.

I dialed the number with shaky fingers. Ashley answered.

"Hi, Ashley," I forced myself to speak normally, instead of sounding like I was squeezed tight by a boa constrictor of nerves.

"Hey, Ana," she said. She still sounded like it was no biggie that I was calling her.

I took a huge breath. What I was about to say seemed impossible, but I guess the deal with impossible things is that they only seem impossible *before* you do them. The words found their way out.

"About tomorrow," I said. "I'm in." My pulse quickened. Would she laugh now like it was all a mean joke?

"Cool," she said. "Meet you in the food court around three?"

"Okay," I said. "See you then."

And that was it.

My first official phone conversation with Ashley had lasted about fifteen seconds, but it felt like a zillion years. Suddenly I was exhausted and collapsed onto my bed to recover. A summer nap sounded like heaven now.

Too bad Daz has a sensor that tells him the very *second* I'm trying to relax.

"Hey, loser!" he bellowed, bulldozing into my room.

I moaned, pulling the pillow over my head. "Not now, Daz. I've had a weird day."

If only boys knew about how rough it was to be a girl some days. All this swimsuit shopping and shark touching and fifteen-second nerve-racking phone calls that threatened to give you heart attacks.

Guys have it so easy.

"*Pfft*. You think *you've* had a weird day?" He shoved me over and sprawled on my bed. "I spent all afternoon running away from supermodels," he babbled. "Do you have any idea how hard it is to walk around with this face?"

You know what the funniest thing about living in a zoo is?

How I didn't even realize I was *already* in one before we moved here.

Things That I Thought Would Be Super Cool about Growing Up That Are Turning Out to Suck— Volume 1:

1. The word *prepubescent*. Let's add the word *'puberty'* to that while we're at it. I mean, everyone *knows* that puberty is no picnic. That's why I hear so many adults talk about how they wouldn't go back to middle school if they were given a million bucks. Thanks for the pep talk, guys. But I never thought that it would be *this* confusing. Having enemies like the Sneerers is hard enough, but what are you supposed to do when one of them suddenly sprouts a nice-girl attitude? Why are there no self-help books for almost teens? Or maybe there are, but they're totally cheesebally with lame titles about "our changing bodies." Bleh.

2. Boys. Once again, I was fooled by every single teen movie I've ever seen. I thought when a boy liked you, he asked you out in some big romantic gesture and that was it. Off you go on dates,

holding hands and stuff. Even Daz, who I *know* likes a girl, is pretty much doing diddly-squat about it! And what if you *think* a boy might like you, but he's sort of…weird about it like Kevin? And what about the boys you can't go out with because they're too old (hello, Logan). How can I have room in my brain for all of them, without going completely insane? (I might have just answered my own question, seeing how it's obvious sanity is not my strong suit here. Hrmph.)

3. Girls. Yeah, I know. Pretty much any living human is on this list now. But seriously.

4. Wet suits. Because let's face it. Being able to swim without getting cold? Awesome. But the way my butt looks in one? No thanks.

Chapter 10

Greenland sharks have parasites that live
in their eyes, which cause them to glow in
the dark.

—*Animal Wisdom*

Guh-ross.

Despite the phrase, it is actually not possible to
laugh one's butt off.

But if you'd told me that I would spend an entire
three hours at the mall on a Saturday afternoon with
my sworn enemy, that is probably what I would
have done. Knowing my Anti-Ashley notebook was
in my backpack made me walk a little taller, like if
it all went horribly, I could call it an experiment,

you know? But it didn't stop the gnawing feeling of something eating away at my insides. Maybe I had a tapeworm on top of everything else.

Not only was I volunteering to actually spend time with Ashley, I was shopping for the *least* fun thing to shop for on the face of the planet.

One word: swimwear.

Welcome to the swimsuit store, where every girl's dreams of looking like a supermodel are replaced with a fluorescent-light reality of your own butt getting the biggest wedgie because we *can* send a man to the moon, but nobody can make a suit that doesn't ride up.

Well, not every girl I guess. Ashley doesn't seem to be scared at all.

"Tell me you threw that old blue thing out," Ashley said as I found her in the food court. A crumpled burrito wrapper was on the table in front of her. "Did you eat yet? You want something?"

"No thanks," I said. I think it was the first time I'd seen Ashley eat something that wasn't salad. "And no, I didn't throw it out. I can't until I have a replacement."

She shook her head. "That's no way to live, *Ana*. You'll never throw it out if you have it to fall back on."

Now I was getting life advice.

"Okay, let's do this." She slid out from the booth. "Remind me I want a new skirt too. Once we get your suit situation figured out." She began sauntering away from the table.

"What? We're not going to Clark's?" I pointed to the right. "Clark's is where I've been getting my suits since forever. I know what they have there," I said.

She lifted her chin. "This is exactly why we are *not* going to Clark's. We're going to Aviana's Bikini Hut," she said matter-of-factly. She grabbed my arm and began dragging me.

I yanked away from her. "I am not getting a bikini!" I said. *Not everyone looks like a model, you know*, I thought bitterly.

She gave me a disgusted look. "They sell more than bikinis, freak. Just *trust* me!"

Oh, sure. Trust the girl who would probably tattoo my face with a gigantic "LOSER" sign if she had the chance. What was I *doing* here?

When we stepped into Aviana's, my eyes practically popped out of my head. "There are *so* many swimsuits here! And all of them are *all about the boobs*!" I pointed to a string bikini on display. "This mannequin is probably embarrassed right now. Plus, it's freezing in here." I adjusted the top of the bikini for her, trying to cover her more.

"Oh my God." Ashley slapped my hand away. "Leave the mannequins alone!" she hissed, darting a look around us and smiling apologetically to the lady behind the counter.

"Did you girls need any help?" She sauntered over to us, looking Ashley up and down. Her eyes slid over to me. "Perhaps something for a pool party?" Steel drums and Caribbean style music jangled in the background.

Ashley shook her head. "No, thanks. We're just looking. I'll call you if we need any help." I stared as the lady nodded and went back to her perch by the cash. Normally when salespeople come up to me in stores, I always feel like I need to humor them, so I don't offend anyone. Then they pester me for ages thinking I want their help. Ashley had dismissed this girl like it was no big deal.

"I'm thinking you need something brighter. That dark suit doesn't do you any favors," she said. The hangers clattered on the racks as Ashley dug behind a mannequin and pulled out a hot pink one piece with beading on the chest.

"No way!" I said, backing away.

She narrowed her eyes. "Why? Because it's a girly color?" The swimsuit swayed on its hanger as she hooked it over her wrist.

"No," I said. "When I wear pink, I look like I'm

always blushing," I said finally. I blush enough from actual embarrassment. I didn't need any extra help in that department.

She shook her head. "That's because you're wearing the wrong pink. You have a tan now, so this one will look good." She threw it in her basket and kept walking, leaving me to follow behind her like a lost puppy.

She turned around suddenly, squinting as she leaned closer. "What?" I asked. I put my hand over my mouth. "Do I have food in my teeth or something?" I checked my shirt for rogue animal stains.

"I'm checking to see the color of your eyes, weirdo," she said. "You should try one in this sea blue too." She whipped around and found another suit in a different style, this time in a bright aquamarine blue. "The ruching will help you." She nodded firmly.

"Ruching? What the heck is ruching?" I held up the suit, examining the scrunchy fabric.

"It's this stuff." She touched the fabric that was bunched around the waist. "It helps disguise problem areas. But don't freak out. It's just a good idea to have on a swimsuit, especially if you're wearing a one piece."

I was beginning to feel like one big problem area.

Following Ashley through the store, I stopped to watch her pick up a sheer orange wrap and hold it next to her hips. Scrunching her nose, she returned it to its spot.

Having never been in Aviana's before, I was starting to realize why I preferred department stores. Some of their stuff was nice, but between the glarey saleslady and the skimpy bikinis on the mannequins, I felt like my clothes were peeling away with each step, leaving me standing vulnerable and naked. I tugged at the bottom of my shirt anxiously.

"Ooh!" Ashley exclaimed. "Here we go! This is perfect. Try this one on." She grabbed me by the shoulders and steered me to the dressing room, with a teal green swimsuit over her shoulder.

"What? Already? We just got here!" I cried. I would sell my firstborn to get out of this.

Ashley stood with her hand on her hip. She wasn't having any of it, I knew that much. "This isn't brain surgery," she said. "You have to actually, you know, *try them on*."

"What if it doesn't fit?" I asked, biting my nails.

"Then we get another size, duh," she said, slapping my hand down.

I stepped inside the fitting room and closed the door, while Ashley flung the suits over the top. "Don't forget the squat test," she yelled.

"The what?" I felt like I was stuck in a test tube. Any minute now the scientists would be here with their goggles to measure how much of a fool I was in here.

"The squat test." Her foot tapped outside the door, with her shoes clicking against the cold floor. "Life is all about the squat test, Ana. You can't expect everything to magically *fit*. You have to try stuff on, and squat, and bend over, and wave your arms and make sure nothing looks weird."

I frowned at the pile of suits hanging in front of me. I guess it made sense. Usually when something didn't fit me, I got annoyed and felt like a weirdly shaped android. But technically, I did the squat test with all sorts of things in my life, so why not clothes? I read the first few pages of a book before deciding if I wanted to buy it. I nibbled on a slice of pizza to see if I liked it.

I took a deep breath and yanked off my shorts and T-shirt. The lights in the fitting room were bright, so I flinched at the off-green zombie that stared back at me. Is that really how my knees look?

Just try on the suit, Ana. It's a swimsuit. It cannot hurt you.

I stepped into the pink suit and pulled it up over my underwear. Honestly, is there anything *less* attractive than wearing a bathing suit WITH your underwear? I know they have that rule so people don't dirty the suits, but why can't somehow invent a way to make this process a little less mortifying? Sliding the straps over my shoulders, I did a test squat. The antitheft knobbie-thing was digging into my collarbone. I waved my arms and even did a little boogie, shaking my butt around.

Hmm.

"You okay in there?" Ashley's voice rang in from outside the door. "Does it fit?"

"I don't know," I said. "The top feels a little weird." I slumped against the wall, hugging my shoulders. The sinking feeling in my chest got worse as Ashley knocked on the door again. This was a stupid idea.

"Well, open up. I'll see what's wrong with it," she said.

At that moment, an alarm went off in my head. *This* would be a perfect opportunity for her to get me good. All it would take is one picture of me in this awful pink eyesore and she could ruin my life.

I hesitated, with my hand stuck in midair by the lock.

"Well?"

I didn't know what to do. My heart was racing, sending a flurry of confusion through me. Being my brave self was so much easier without swimsuits.

Okay.

Taking a deep breath, I opened the door. I braced for the worst.

But it was only Ashley.

No camera. No phone. No anything. She had another pile of suits in her basket.

"Hmm, I see what you mean." She reached up and adjusted the strap, giving it a tug. "It's too tight. It's because you're taller than it's made for," she said. She pursed her glossy lips. "I think we should get it in a size up. It's a bit snug on the chest anyway, so it will probably work."

She disappeared back into the racks before I could argue.

"Here, try this one. They didn't have pink, but that nice blue you like was in." She handed me the blue suit in a different size.

I clenched my teeth as I tried it on. I wanted to go home, but I was also curious if Ashley's method was going to work. Beads of sweat began to collect on my forehead. Pulling the straps over my shoulders, I squeezed my eyes shut.

It's just a swimsuit.

"Knock, knock," Ashley said. "That must be better."

I opened the door again.

"Oh. My. *God*," Ashley said. I winced, but she was beaming. "Do a turn! It fits so well! I *told you* blue was your color! And look how well it fits!" She yanked me from the fitting room to the gigantic mirror at the end of the hallway. I hunched over, trying to hide myself and avoid the prying eyes of other shoppers, but nobody seemed to notice. The floor was cold under my bare feet.

"You like it?" I asked hesitantly. With the three-way mirror in front of me, it was hard not to stare at myself. To pick out every flaw. My weird-looking knees. The uneven tan on my arms. My lack of a butt. But somehow, this suit made them a little harder to spot. The blue made my eyes stand out, and somehow it contrasted with my hair to make it look extra shiny. I looked like *me*, but now I was a shiny, better version. Maybe even a *kissable* version?

"Like it?" Ashley gaped at me. "You're buying it. I don't care if you have to sell a kidney or a snake or get your rich grandpa to send you a check. You're buying that." She crossed her arms over her chest.

I felt the corners of my mouth turn up.

"I probably wouldn't have tried it on," I admitted. "I mean, after the first one didn't fit."

Ashley waved her hand dismissively. "Just remember, if something doesn't fit, that's the *clothes'* fault. Not yours. Keep trying things on until you find something that looks like it was made for you. Everything in your closet should make you feel good."

"I never really thought about it," I said.

Something was swirling in my stomach, but I couldn't pinpoint the feeling. "Spending so much time trying to look good…" I trailed off.

"What? You think it's shallow to want to look good?" Her eyes hardened.

"No!" I exclaimed, suddenly freaked out. "Well. I don't know. I always sort of figured you looked great in everything and were trying to rub it in." I could feel the heat crawl up my neck. "You know?"

She scoffed. "Please. You're dead wrong on that one. You should see me in lavender. I look like a zombie."

Ashley breezed past me, grabbing a pair of short shorts from the rack. "I'm going to try these on," she said. "I got some shirts too, so wander around and see if there's anything else you like." She stepped into the fitting room beside mine while I ducked back into mine to change.

As I stepped back into my comfy shorts and shirt, it occurred to me that this little shopping trip with Ashley was a sort of squat test of its own. And so far, I was eerily surprised by how it was turning out. I mean, she was *trying* to help, wasn't she?

Who knew that if clothes didn't fit you, it *wasn't* because you were some sort of freak? And could anyone have guessed that underneath that sneery, snarky exterior, Ashley was an actual person?

"So what's going on with you and that geek guy?" she yelled from her fitting room. "Is that officially a thing yet or what?"

"Who? Kevin? You know who he is?" I stuck my tongue out at her door. "We've gone to school together forever." I fiddled with the antitheft tag on my swimsuit and hung the rejects on the rack outside the room.

"Blah, blah. Spill it," she said. I could tell she was smiling inside the room.

"Nothing. We're just friends."

"Oh, come on," Ashley said. "I've seen the way you guys were at school. And you went to the dance together, and he totally stares at you all the time, *and* you stare right back at him looking all awkward and dopey."

Great. So the entire world knew then.

"I mean it. We went to the dance as a group, with some other friends."

"And your brother," she piped in.

"Yes, him too."

"He's kind of cute, you know," she said. I frowned at the closed fitting room door.

"Who? Kevin? Or my brother?" I couldn't help but cringe.

"Well, both of them," she said. "Your brother is a nutcase, though. But Kevin is cute, if you like the whole nerdy guy thing. That's not exactly my type. But I can see how he could be *someone's* type, you know?"

"I think he's really hot," I admitted, blushing. "Plus, he's smart and nice, and that makes him seem even hotter." I glanced at myself in the mirror again, surprised by the smile on my face.

"You guys gone out yet?" Ashley asked. "You know, on a *date*." The word took up a lot of space in the room.

"That's none of your business!" I squeaked.

"So no, huh?" She giggled from behind the door.

"I didn't say that!"

"You didn't have to," she said. She flung a reject suit over the top of the door. "You should ask him out."

My jaw dropped. This was too surreal. Could she read my mind about the kiss pact or what? I couldn't believe Ashley was giving me boy advice. "You can't just go and…" I fumbled. "Ask people out!" For a moment, I considered spilling the truth about the kiss pact. But surrounded by mannequin boobs and Lycra, my head was already spinning.

"Please," she said. "You *so* can. He's obviously into you. He's probably shy. Lots of geeky guys are shy. So you have to be the one to make the first move."

I shook my head furiously. "No way. I could never do that." It occurred to me that if I couldn't even ask Kevin out, I probably didn't have the guts to full on kiss him either. *Argh.*

"I dunno," she said in a singsongy voice. "You also said you'd never wear pink."

"I'll think about it," I said.

Part of me liked the idea of making the first move for the kiss pact. It would mean I wouldn't have to sit around wondering if Kevin liked me for real. I *always* feel like there's something we're not saying. You know how in comics there are always thought bubbles rising above the people? I always feel like there's a thought bubble above Kevin's head, but I can never see what's in it.

Maybe his thought bubble is, *Hey, Ana, I like you too.* But for all I know, he could be thinking, *Hey, can you get me a cheese sandwich?*

Who knows with boys?

"Coming out," Ashley announced. She opened the door and came out wearing a new green shirt. "What do you think? I like how it looks with my hair, but is the back sort of funny?" She swung around so I could look.

I inspected it. "Nope, it looks good. It fits great."

"Cool. I want to look extra good for Logan for the opening!" She pranced back inside to change. "He's got to get sick of that two-faced Danielle girl someday," she sang out cheerfully.

I snorted. "Still convinced you're going to marry him and have a zillion babies?"

"It's going to be a June wedding," she said, her voice muffled under her shirt as she changed.

The door swung open one last time, and she stepped out in her regular clothes. "Ready? We can pay for these and go to Jane's for some cute hair accessories or something."

"I thought we were only getting suits?" I asked.

She shrugged. "This is fun. I haven't been here in a while," she said. "Ever since Brooke and Rayna practically ditched me for the summer."

The mention of the other Sneerers' names hit me like sharp gravel. I'd forgotten about them. And any time Ashley was around them, she became a monster. My lip curled automatically as I pictured their faces.

"Where did they go?" I asked as Ashley piled her clothes onto the checkout counter. Brazil? San Diego? The moon?

I could only hope.

Ashley scoffed as the cashier rang her up. Ashley handed over a credit card. "Rayna's dad has some horse training farm thing in Nebraska, and Brooke's parents took her with them on a trip to Florida to visit her brother in college." She clicked her tongue. "For the entire summer," she spat.

"Huh…" I said. I would have look delighted I

bet, except Ashley's eyes were suddenly super sad. Her lip quivered.

"Hey," I said. "It's okay. They'll be back for school. I know it sucks when friends go away." I thought of Liv going off on her first date. How I wouldn't be around to see the look on her face when she got back to tell me all about it. "Summer's practically almost over. It will go fast, and besides, you've got sharks to keep you occupied." I shoved her shoulder awkwardly.

She nodded and shook her head once, sniffing. The sad look on her face disappeared instantly, and her eyes turned hard again. I was amazed at how quick she could do that. Usually when I'm sad, I couldn't hide it even if I had a bag over my head. "You're right. The sharks are pretty fun," she said. "Do you and Liv still talk a lot?"

"A little bit," I said. "It's hard, though. There's a big time difference, and…" I trailed off. "And she's making a lot of new friends. That's good, I guess," I said. Probably more to myself.

"Well, so are you," Ashley said. She scooped up her bag and swung it. "Hurry up." She pointed to the credit card machine, which was waiting for the card I'd borrowed from Dad.

I drummed on my backpack with my fingers, feeling the hard cover of my Anti-Ashley notebook inside. I hadn't needed it yet. This was probably the first time in our lives we'd had an entire conversation that didn't *feel* weird. Almost like we were two normal friends, hanging out and trying on swimsuits. Was this the first time I "squat tested" Ashley as a friend?

"Ooh, we can grab some ice cream too. Mint chocolate chip, here I come." Ashley rubbed her hands together and narrowed her eyes like a sneaky villain.

I swiped my card.

Ice cream sounded great.

Chapter 11

Giant clams are the largest mollusks on earth, weighing up to five hundred pounds and reaching four feet in length.

—*Animal Wisdom*

Five hundred pounds?! I'm never going in the ocean again.

Sharks in swimsuits. Crocodiles in short shorts. Starfish doing the squat test.

That is what I spent all night dreaming about, thanks to my shopping day with Ashley. It was like my brain took all the worries in my head, threw them in an empty mayonnaise jar, and shook them all up together in some colossal, murky mess of swimsuit anxiety and frenemy fear. Why couldn't I dream about skating on a chocolate chip cookie or something?

I was almost afraid to see Ashley at the zoo the following Monday. We'd had actual *fun* together, but I couldn't shake the edgy feeling that the whole thing was a setup or some sort of sugar-high fantasy that I'd concocted on my own after eating too many Golden Grahams.

But the beautiful new swimsuit hanging off my closet doorknob was proof. So was the buggy-eyed look on Dad's face when I showed him the receipt from Aviana's Bikini Hut. Trust him to not understand that ruching and "fake-a-butt" fabric doesn't come cheap.

Swimsuit or not, it seemed like it would only take one false move on my part for Ashley to morph back to her Sneerer self. I didn't want to make any mistakes, so I planned my entrance down to the letter before showing up to the Adventure Zone to work together again. I would just walk in calmly, act completely natural like it *wasn't* a huge deal that we'd hung out and did squat tests together, and say, "Hey."

It was foolproof.

Ashley was in the changing room, finishing off her cup of yogurt with her blue notebook propped open on her lap. She didn't look like she'd dreamed about sharks or any other sea creatures in swimsuits. In fact, Ashley looked as put together as always. Her hair was back in a sleek ponytail, and her eyelids twinkled with gold shimmers.

"Hey, Ana," she said, standing up and tossing her cup into the garbage can. She washed her spoon in the tiny fountain and wiped it on the hem of her shirt before stuffing it into her locker. "Did your dad flip about the suit?" she asked.

"Only a little," I said, relieved she was still being nice. Not *exactly* the truth, but I didn't want to seem like a total loser with uptight parents now.

"Thanks again," I added, taking the chance while I had it. "For the swimsuit stuff, I mean. I tried it on again this morning and still really love it," I said.

She didn't need to know that I *might* have also strutted around my room to music, trying to look like one of those models on the beach in the summery commercials. Actually, *no one* needed to know that.

Ashley grinned. "Told ya," she said. "I like mine too. It will help when we're presenting at the grand opening event, I bet. Good clothes *always* boost my confidence." She dug into her pocket and pulled out a tube of shimmery peach gloss. "Just like lip gloss," she added, slicking some over her lips.

Something about Ashley's easygoing attitude today and the perfectly applied lip gloss made the question flicker in my mind again. She'd helped with the swimsuit. Maybe she would help with the whole kiss pact thing now? Could I trust her? I was about to open my mouth and spill the beans about it when Patricia ducked her head into the room.

"Ana! Great, you're here," she said, bustling inside. She looked even more frazzled than normal, with her hair sticking out in frizzy bits all over her head. Her eyebrows were furrowed with concern. "We need to *talk* before you two get to work today."

Ashley and I darted a look at each other, trying to figure out what was coming. I hated it when adults said, "We need to talk." It's basically like saying, "We need to eat this rotting egg salad sandwich," or "We need to pluck all your leg hairs out one by one." It never ends well.

"Okay," I said, gritting my teeth. "What's up?"

Patricia waited a beat before speaking. "There's been a bit of a mix-up, I'm afraid," she said. She looked anxiously at the fridge. "You're both familiar with the feeding procedures for the sea horses, correct?" She looked from me to Ashley.

I frowned. What was she getting at? "Y-yes," I said. "The babies get the live brine shrimp, and the older ones get shrimps and copepods." Holding my breath, I checked with Ashley. She nodded curtly, wringing her hands.

"Well, for some reason they were overfed last Friday, nearly triple what they need," she said. The lines around her mouth deepened with worry. "I cleaned out the tank this morning, and it doesn't matter *who* did it," she said, emphasizing her words by slowing them down, like she was talking to kindergartners. "I want you both to make sure you're extra clear you're not both doing it and mixing up the amounts."

Ashley seemed to shrink as I turned to her. She was in charge of the sea horses last time. Her hair made a curtain between us as she dipped her head lower.

"But, Ms. Shurman," Ashley blurted. "I was *so* careful when I fed them, I swear! I measured twice and everything." Her face was turning pink as she spoke.

I stood there, silent. I could remember exactly when Ashley had fed the sea horses last time. It was the same day we went shopping, and she had put in the right amount, I'd thought.

But had I missed something? Did she overfeed them?

Patricia didn't seem convinced. "Well, *someone* accidentally put too much food in there, so make sure that you keep the lines of communication open. We can't have mistakes like that because the animals could get hurt. And, Ana." She looked to me.

I flinched hearing my name, with hot shame

rising up traitorously to my face. "I'm trusting *you* to be extra careful, okay? Ashley is new here, so she may not be used to the basics yet. But you've been working in the zoo for ages, so you should know better. Always double-check!"

The words pricked against me like porcupine quills.

You should know better.

I swallowed thickly as Ashley stared at her feet.

"Yes, ma'am," I squeaked, straining against my tightening throat. It didn't seem fair, blaming me for one of Ashley's accidents. But...what if it *wasn't* an accident? Ashley wouldn't put animals in danger like that, would she? No, it had to have been an honest mistake.

"Excellent. On to business." Patricia clapped, signaling she was out of "stern" mode and back into "let's-get-some-work-done" mode. "Before you start today, I wanted to make sure you were familiar with the new cage protocol on some of the small creatures here." She pointed to the tank of crabs that lined the lower west wall of the exhibit.

"The backs of the cages all have waterproof note-books attached to the doors." She pointed to the hanging notepads. "Every time you open or close a cage, you sign in and out, okay? Use this red pencil," she added. "It's waterproof."

"Okay," Ashley said. I was still too mortified at Patricia's lecture to talk.

"It keeps everything sorted here and gets us in the habit of double-checking all the locks," Patricia explained. "Don't worry. You'll get the hang of it quickly," she said, waving us off to do our chores while she shuffled back into her tiny office.

Patricia's lecture kept playing over and over in my head as Ashley and I set to work for the afternoon.

You should know better.

Four little words, but they felt like weights clinging to me. Was there any worse feeling than shame? It seemed to squirrel away inside of you, popping its head out whenever you *think* you're fine and over something. Like a rabid rodent inside your heart waiting for you to feel okay about yourself so *POOF*, it can magically reappear and make you feel like crap all over again.

I couldn't help but notice that Ashley's easygoing, happy attitude had also faded. Instead, she cleaned all the glass on the outside of the tanks with hardly a word, focusing on each and every stroke of her paper towel. Even her bright green fingernails seemed duller.

"I didn't do it," she said finally, lifting her feet one at a time so I could run the wet mop over the floor around her.

I looked up. "The sea horse thing?" I asked. "You can tell me if you make a mistake. It's totally okay." I tried to be patient and reassure her, sort of the way Mom does when I accidentally put one of my red shirts in with Dad's white shirts in the washing machine and turn the whole load into a hot mess of bubblegum pink. I tried to make her know that even if she *had* messed up, it was fine.

She bit her lip and shook her head adamantly. "No, I mean it! I double-checked it and definitely did *not* add three times as much! I'd have to be insane to do that!"

I shrugged. "It can happen! I once accidentally fed Darwin cornflakes because I wasn't paying attention. I practically had the milk poured over him before I realized." I grimaced at the memory. Darwin didn't let me live that down for months, always flinching when I walked up to him with a glass of milk.

But Ashley glared at me. "I'm telling you, Ana. I did *not* mess up."

I let out a slow breath. "Well, someone did!" I said, throwing my hands up. The anger surged higher. "And I got blamed for it, so…" I shook my head, breathing out a lungful of frustrated air. This was stupid. I didn't want to argue over something so dumb.

"I didn't want you to get blamed," Ashley said,

jutting out her chin. "I'm just telling you I didn't do it!"

I clamped my mouth shut. To me, it seemed perfectly clear that Ashley had made a mistake. I mean, food doesn't magically *appear* in sea horse tanks, you know? It was her job last time, so it definitely wasn't me. So why couldn't she own up to it? Was she trying to say she thought *I'd* done it?

I finished mopping, taking my frustrations out on the floor.

Ashley didn't say anything as I put the mop away, signed my name on the checkout sheet, and loaded up my backpack to head home for the day. She didn't respond when I sighed loudly trying to get her attention, and she didn't answer when I pushed the locker room door open and held it for her as she rushed ahead of me and bolted outside.

"Bye then," I muttered, watching her dart away. She disappeared fast into the crowd of visitors, but I didn't miss how quickly her hand reached up to wipe her eyes. Was she crying? Or was it all for show to make me feel bad for her?

Inside my backpack, the Anti-Ashley notebook weighed heavily on my shoulders as I wordlessly tied my shoes before leaving. Should I write about the sea horse mishap, to be safe? I didn't know.

It was starting to feel like the most obvious

things—even Ashley being a Sneerer—weren't so black and white anymore. It reminded me of zebras somehow. Like I was always used to seeing them with their black-and-white stripes, just like I was always used to Ashley acting like a jerk. But now? Not being *sure* that Ashley was sabotaging me?

That was like seeing a herd of gray zebras.

Were they even zebras without their stripes?

And was Ashley *Ashley* without her mean?

Chapter 12

Penguins don't have teeth, but they do have fleshy spines that face backward in their mouths that guide fish down their throats.

—*Animal Wisdom*

well, that's a lovely image to consider right before I eat anything ever again.

"These cookies taste like cardboard," Bella announced. Her short hair was flecked with bits of flour, and there was a smear of molasses on her cheek. Ever since we'd been recruited as her "official kitchen helpers" for her upcoming bake sale at the old-age home, Kevin, Daz, and I had seen a whole new side of Bella.

And it was pretty funny.

Even though she took baking *crazy* seriously.

Daz leaped to his feet. "No, they don't!" He grabbed one from the huge pile on the counter and shoved the whole thing in his mouth. "They're *thuper tasthy*," he mumbled, spraying crumbs. "*Mmm, stho good!*" His eyes widened, and he nodded eagerly. I didn't miss the look of regret in his eyes as he tried to swallow.

I'd tried one of the cookies.

I'd also spat it out into a napkin when Bella wasn't looking.

Bella sighed. "They are not! They taste like sawdust and cardboard had a baby and covered it with seeds!" She threw a wadded-up paper towel into the garbage. "How am I going to feed a bunch of senior citizens these?! They'll break their dentures!" She wheeled around, staring at Kevin.

"Hey, they're not that bad. They're not quite as good as the no-bake ones, though," he admitted. "But they really do taste okay." He tried to nonchalantly lean away from the pile of warm cookies that Daz was offering him.

Bella pouted. It made her elfish features stand out even more. "Do you think I should add more sugar?" she asked desperatcly. She stirred the bowl of porridgelike goo in her hands. The mass was beginning to stick to the spoon, making it noticeably hard for her to mix. Beads of sweat were popping up over her eyebrows.

I cleared my throat. "Maybe it's best we try another recipe entirely," I said. I gently took the bowl from her and set it on the table. I didn't know much about baking, but I was pretty sure I could recognize "edible cement" when I saw it.

Picking up the medieval cookbook, I flipped to the table of contents. "There must be something here that's super quick. Here, how about this?" I held up the picture. "What about fruit kebabs in honey? That sounds good."

"That will spoil, I think," Bella said dully.

I kept flipping, while Kevin leaned over my shoulder to read. A buzz of heat ran through my face. Did he *know* how close he was? I mean, I could just turn my head and...

"Hey," he said. He pointed to the page, brushing his hand against mine.

Stay cool.

"How about this?" he asked. "Candied sweet potatoes." He looked up to Bella for her opinion.

She chewed on her lip. "Do you think that would be good? Sounds kind of..." she trailed off.

"Like candied potatoes," Daz offered, his nose crinkling. "No thanks." The two of them giggled, sharing a glance. *Oh, please.* The last thing we needed now was the two of them getting all schmoopy-lovey. At least I *tried* to not trip all over Kevin, even though he looked adorable and kept smiling with that dimple in his left cheek.

"*I* think it would be good," I said, lifting my chin. "We always have sweet potatoes with nuts and marshmallow fluff on the top at Thanksgiving. It tastes *amazing*. Plus, they wouldn't break their dentures, so…"

Daz snored. "Bor-rinnnggg."

But Bella perked up. "You know, you might be right!" She wiped the molasses on her cheek and grimaced. "Sweet potatoes could work, and I know we have a lot of them in the pantry. Hold on a sec." She scurried off to grab the potatoes. "At least there are no seeds in them!" she yelled back.

Twenty minutes later, because of Kevin's brilliant idea, the sweet potatoes were boiling on the stove. The whole kitchen smelled like cinnamon and orange zest. Bella put Daz and Kevin to work measuring spices, while the two of us kept peeling more potatoes.

"So how's it going with the man-eating monster?" Bella asked, shoving a handful of potato skins in the garbage. "And the sharks? How are they doing?" She grinned at her own joke.

For some reason, I couldn't force a laugh out of myself. "Ashley is okay," I said. A warm feeling settled over my chest as I realized that Bella might have been right about Ashley from the start. She could just want to move on with our lives. "It's been sort of fun. We even went shopping together for swimsuits on Saturday." I braced myself for her reaction. If I told Liv that I went shopping with Ashley, she'd probably shriek so loud she'd blow out an eardrum and accuse me of moving to the dark side.

But thankfully, Bella wasn't like that.

"That's awesome," she said. "Maybe when school starts you guys won't hate each other so much," she mused. "It would probably make school better."

I stopped peeling my potato. It suddenly felt heavy in my hand. "I don't know," I said. "It's hard to imagine her outside of the zoo, you know? I think she actually *likes* it, and it's weird to think of her being nice if she's not there." I considered what going back to school might be like and running into Ashley in the halls. Would she go back to hating me?

A rusty orange curl of potato dropped to the counter beneath my peeler. "Actually, something sort of happened today," I admitted. "And I'm not sure what to think."

Bella grabbed another potato. "Something bad?"

I kept my eyes down, focusing on the bumpy

skin. "There's this sea horse tank, right? And it's been Ashley's job to feed them. When we got there, though, Patricia said that *someone* had overfed them. By a lot." I cringed.

Bella's eyes widened. "Were they okay?" She tossed another potato into a pot. "The sea horses, I mean. I always thought those things were so cute."

"Oh! Yeah, they're going to be fine. But the point is, Ashley had been doing that job for a while now, and it was, like, *three times* the food they need. It was weird." I paused, feeling the shame creep up on me again without warning. "And Patricia sort of blamed me for it in a way. She said I should know better and that I should be watching out for Ashley because she's newer."

I couldn't keep my lip from curling.

Bella tapped the peeler against her potato. "And you think maybe Ashley did it on purpose? Or…?"

I huffed. "I don't know! It just seemed sort of crummy, you know? Like, Patricia giving *me* a lecture because of something that was so clearly Ashley's fault!"

Bella nodded. "That does suck. But what if someone else put in the food?"

I lifted my shoulders. "It's only us and Patricia and Logan in there right now. It's not like Logan did it. He needs his job for school. The worst part is,

Ashley wouldn't even admit that she did it. It wasn't even a *possibility* that she'd screwed up," I mumbled.

I watched Bella carefully, trying to read her reaction. But in true Bella fashion, she kept her opinions hidden beneath her thoughtful face. Finally, she wiped her hands on her apron. "It sounds to me like Ashley made an honest mistake," she said. "But she didn't want to admit it."

I brightened. "You think? I don't really know what to do. I *like* that we can sort of hang out together now and Ashley isn't a horrible monster. But if she's going to be sneaking around trying to mess things up for me—"

"No, I don't think that's it at all," Bella interrupted. "If it was her in charge of feeding them, and no one else can get in there, it *had* to be her mistake. She's probably afraid to fess up because she feels dumb messing up in front of you."

My jaw dropped. "In front of *me*? You have to be kidding. I'm *always* messing up!"

"Ain't that the truth!" Daz yelped suddenly from the living room. Now that the spices were organized, he and Kevin had abandoned the kitchen. I was fairly certain they were building a robot, by the clinking and ripping sounds going on out there. I glared at him while Bella giggled. *Stupid boys.*

"I mean it!" Bella said. "Think about it. At school,

she's super popular and can pretty much do whatever she wants and she's still going to be cool. But at the zoo? That's your territory." She set the pot of potatoes over by the sink and made bunny quotes in the air with her fingers. "The granddaughter of the *great* Shep Foster!"

I made a face.

"It's true! I remember when I first found out I was a little freaked," she admitted.

"You were?" That didn't seem like Bella at all. She was too busy being stealthy behind her atlases and notebooks at school to worry about me.

"Definitely. But then I got to know you and realized that even though your grandpa is famous, you're still pretty much a basket case." She elbowed me teasingly.

"Ha. Ha."

"You done with those potatoes yet? It's almost time to switch them! This batch is done!" Daz called over again. He and Kevin appeared with a tissue-box monster they'd made that had a paper-towel-roll minion, with forks for legs. It was beyond me how Daz could make fun of me for sketching in a notebook "like a loser" (his words), but here he was basically making craft monsters like a bizarre boy version of Martha Stewart.

"We'd better make sure they don't mess this

up." Bella sighed, pulling her bowl of potatoes from the counter.

As I dumped the steaming hot potatoes into the colander, I thought Bella was probably right about Ashley—it was an honest mistake, and I could make things a whole lot better between us by letting it go. Already the weight of the whole thing seemed to be lifting away from me.

"You okay?" Kevin asked, as I helped Bella add sugar and cloves into the pot of potatoes. "You seem a little distracted." His hair was doing that supercute "flip-into-his-eyes" thing that made my heart tap-dance.

"I'm okay now," I said, smiling. "Just trying to avoid the potato sauna." I blew at the hot steam, pushing thoughts of Ashley out of my head.

"Don't forget," Daz announced. He had a stick of cinnamon tucked behind his ear like a pen, trying to look official. There was a haughty grin on his face. "Tomorrow. The old-age center. *We ride at dawn!*" He lifted his fist to the air and hooted like a warrior.

Bella shook her head, trying not to giggle. "Actually it's not till 6:00 p.m.," she said quietly. "And we don't have to, uh…ride. We just need to show up so you can all help me set up."

Daz blinked. "*At dawn!*"

Kevin and I ignored him. "We'll be there," I promised. "I'll even bring some art stuff, so we can make up some cool signs for you."

Kevin nodded. "You've got my calculator for sales," he said.

"*And my ax!*" Daz bellowed.

Sometimes staying sane with my brother around is like trying to whistle with a mouthful of crackers.

Impossible.

And messy.

Chapter 13

Clown fish are immune to sea anemone
stings because they are protected by a layer
of mucus.

—*Animal Wisdom*

This just in: I'm super glad not to be a clown fish. Can you imagine walking around trying to live your life covered in mucus? It's bad enough I smell like dead fish half the time.

The next day felt like the summer had turned a brand-new page. Usually, I wake up when Darwin climbs on my head and shoves his bird butt in my face.

But today? There was nothing but the sun streaming through my curtains, along with that warm-fruity-cantaloupe breeze that only happens on those *perfect* summer days when there are *no* bird butts in your face. Somehow, the air felt *bigger* in my lungs.

It was heaven.

It's funny how some girl talk and a good night of sleep can make the world seem sane again. Even the lions outside my window seemed extra mellow, rolling over onto their backs and pawing at the air like gigantic kittens as I peered out at them.

I was still feeling good when I showed up at the Adventure Zone that morning. Even Patricia seemed to be extra happy, and there was no sign on her face that she was still upset about the sea horse incident. All was forgotten, and Ashley showed up looking as normal and sparkly as ever, with her hair up in a poofy bun and gold earrings in her ears.

It was actually nice to see she was okay, and I felt a surge of happiness knowing I didn't write about the awful sea horse thing in my notebook.

Everybody had bad days, right?

"I've got a glamorous job for you ladies today," Patricia said when I walked into the locker room. By the look of her devious grin I could tell that *glamour* probably wasn't the right word for it. Hopefully it wouldn't involve poop. That was the last thing I wanted on a non-bird-butt day like this.

Ashley looked up. "More memorizing notes?"

she asked, holding up her notebook. "My notebook is practically full."

"Nope," Patricia said. "Once you're done with your regular feedings, we just got some extra shells in for the education tables. That's the good news."

"And the bad news?" I asked. Please don't say we have to clean them or something else totally boring.

Patricia winked. "The bad news is, they're not sorted. And they need to be." She pulled out a chart from her back pocket, unfolding the paper. Shells of different shapes and colors were drawn all over, categorized by type.

"That's a lot of shells," Ashley said, dumb-founded. "I thought shells were just...shells?" She took the poster and examined it.

"Then this will be good for you." Patricia patted her on the back. "Can't have a shark girl thinking all shells are the same, can we? I need you girls to clean them off, sort through them, and put them in the right containers. They're already set up here." She showed us over to the education table and pointed out the rows of bowls, each labeled with a variety of shell names. "Everything from angel wings to scallops to murex shells is in here," she said proudly.

"What's a murex shell?" Ashley asked. She peered over to look into the empty container.

"That's for you to find out!" Patricia said, waving us to work.

After doing our usual chores and feedings, Ashley and I grabbed some chairs, parked ourselves at the table, and gawked at the forty gazillion shells in front of us.

"Did you have any idea that there were so many *shells*?" Ashley asked, narrowing her eyes at a pearly pink scallop shell. She cleaned it with a damp paper towel and checked the legend on the chart, putting it in its proper place.

It's funny how you don't realize that there are different versions of your own life. There's the version where you worry about people spilling chicken parm on you at lunch. Then there's the life where you sit with your sworn enemy and sort shells. I know which one *I* liked better.

Once Ashley and I got down to business, a calm settled over the room. The crystal blue water of the tanks around us reflected bright lights and shadows along the blue walls, and the raucous sounds of the zoo outside became silent. All we could hear was the gentle hum of the tanks. There were no weird questions about boys. There were no sea horse emergencies. There were no kiss pacts. Just two girls who might possibly be friends and a bucket of shells.

"So has this summer made you want to be a

mermaid or what?" Ashley said a little while later, stretching her arms above her head. She yawned widely.

I shook my head. "It's really fun, but I'm more of a crocodile girl," I said. I double-checked a lightning whelk and set it into its pile. "There's a lot less teeth with these things, at least." I held up another shell to the light. "Hey, look how cool this one is." I handed her a shiny, spirally shell with cool ridges. "I think it's a…" I looked down again at the legend.

"Brown-band wentletrap," Ashley finished for me. "I *like* that there's nothing here to bite us today," she said, smirking. Her eyes were brighter than I'd ever seen them. Maybe this was all some strange sea-magic making her nice. I didn't want it to end. I was starting to realize that being enemies was *tiring*.

"Oh! First murex shell!" I held it up. "Now we're officially smart enough to be here." I laughed. Ashley took it to examine it.

"Wow," she breathed. "Think Patricia would let me take one home?" She held it to the light.

"I don't know," I said. "Hang on." I dug around the pile some more, coming up with a handful of other murex shells. "It's not the only one. I don't think she'd mind. I won't tell her," I added in a hushed voice.

Ashley beamed, pocketing the shell.

"This thing says that some shells are either

left- or right-handed," she said. Flipping a junonia shell in her hands, she furrowed her brows. "But how the heck can you tell? Is this left-handed?" She held up the shell. "Or this?" she asked, swiveling it around.

I looked at the diagram. It was a confusing mess of arrows and counterclockwise this and clockwise that, wrapped around a 3-D image of a shell. "Uh, pretty sure the only way you can tell if they're right- or left-handed is to hand them a pen." I snorted.

Ashley rolled her eyes, but that didn't stop her from laughing. I pocketed a periwinkle shell because I liked the name. It was almost like it tickled your tongue to say it.

We sorted shells like that for what seemed like hours, but it had been only forty-five minutes by the time the last shell was in its pile. Ashley was happier than I'd ever seen her. Of course, she got even happier when Logan appeared behind us.

"Look at you!" he said, leaning over to check out the shell piles. "Didn't you guys just get here? How did you finish sorting so quickly?"

A blossom of pride grew inside me, seeing how impressed he was.

Ashley sat straighter and brushed her hair from her face. "We're talented, I guess," she said. Then her face dropped when she saw Danielle tagging along behind him. Her dark ponytail swung behind her like a pendulum as she moved.

"Hey, girls! Great to see you!" Her voice was weird and too familiar, like she was trying to make it sound like we'd been friends forever. Ashley must have noticed too because she quirked her eyebrow at me in question.

"Hi, Danielle," I said, forcing myself to be polite. Just because she got to hang off a Sun God didn't mean I could be rude to her.

Even though I kind of wanted to stick out my tongue out of spite.

"How have you girls been lately?" she asked, slipping her hand into Logan's. I tried not to stare as her fingertips tightened around his hand. "It's been ages since I've seen you!" She dragged the words out as a whine, acting like she was upset about it. Was she trying to look good in front of Logan or what?

"Oh, you know," I said. "Working hard, sorting shells." I pointed to our growing display.

"We had to learn what *all* of these shells are," Ashley said curtly, settling back in her chair and crossing her arms.

Logan whistled. "That's a lot," he admitted. "Pretty sure if it doesn't have teeth, I won't be able to remember its name." He exaggerated a frown as Danielle reached up and poked his shoulder.

"That's because you're obsessed with your *sharks*." She giggled.

Oh Lord, not with the giggling now.

I glanced at Ashley and rolled my eyes the teensiest bit so only she could see. I was starting to see why Ashley had called her a two-face. There *was* something about her that seemed *too something*. Too nice? Too interested? Too *sparkly*? Why was she here so much anyway? Could she not bear to be away from Logan for that long or what?

Logan continued. "Well, you must be doing a great job. I've heard nothing but good things from Patricia. You must be psyched for Saturday, huh?" he said, leaning in close so he could fake-whisper without Patricia hearing. It made his hair fall over his eyes exactly the way Kevin's does that makes my heart go into a little spasmy-beat-skip thing.

I fumbled with another murex shell and dropped it into place in its jar.

Danielle kept yammering. "You guys should be so proud. Seriously, when I was your age, there was no way I'd be able to do something with so much responsibility."

There was a weird intense glimmer in her eyes as she spoke. What did Logan see in this girl anyway? Besides the whole porcelain-skin, Pantene-commercial-hair thing, I mean.

Logan wrapped his arm around her shoulder. "We should get out of here, babe. I'm sure these two want to get their lunch."

"Bye, guys!" Ashley said, eyeing the door so Danielle would get the hint.

Logan gave us a thumbs-up as he went through the door to the back room with Danielle in tow. "You're going to be a great team for the kids," he added.

At least I think that's what he said because I might have gotten a little distracted by the way he held the door for Danielle like a gentleman on their way out.

"Thanks!" Ashley said. "I think so too."

Were we a good team?

"Oh my God, that guy is hot," Ashley whispered, leaning back to fan herself with one of the shell pamphlets. Now that Logan was gone, the super-chill attitude was gone, replaced with a fan-girly giggly mess.

"Right?!" I laughed with her. "I think I see your point though about Danielle," I said quietly. "She seems sort of…"

"Yeah," Ashley said smugly. "Told you. That girl is trouble."

I shrugged. "Well, she is if *you* want to marry him, that's for sure," I pointed out with a smile.

Ashley bared her teeth in annoyance. "Sometimes boys make things a lot more difficult than they need to be," she said haughtily.

I thought about Kevin, and how even though it was *possible* he liked me back, it was still like trying to see the future through grape jelly to find out for sure or figure out if I would *ever* get to kiss him. Suddenly the summer seemed like it would be over in seconds, and the kiss pact deadline would be long gone. I'd be left behind as Liv crossed over into "I've-kissed-a-boy" territory.

"No arguments there," I admitted.

Since when did Ashley and I agree on so much?

Chapter 14

Puffer fish are able to gulp huge amounts
of water to blow up into a ball several
times their size to protect themselves
from predators.

—*Animal Wisdom*

Imagine if this was what we did every time we
were afraid. Scared to do a school presentation? Puff up like a balloon. Afraid of getting
your first kiss? Puff up like a balloon. If only
life's problems could be solved by acting like a
puffer fish.

I left the Adventure Zone a little early, telling Ashley
that I must have had some bad milk for breakfast.

But the truth was, the whole thing with Logan and what Ashley had said about boys were making me feel rotten. Sometimes, no matter how much you want to hide from something, it sniffs you out like a hungry raccoon in a garbage can.

I had to face the truth. I hadn't gotten any closer to kissing Kevin. I wasn't even sure if I wanted to. Not that it mattered, because I was *so* not going to let Liv be the only one to kiss a boy this summer.

But no matter how much I thought about it or *wished* for it to happen, my first kiss with Kevin wouldn't happen if I didn't actually *do* something.

So how come I couldn't force myself out of bed?

Whipping my curtains closed to block out the cheery sun, I contemplated the chances of surviving the rest of junior high. I hadn't even hit eighth grade yet and already felt like I was failing somehow.

Was this why all those people in teen movies are always crying? Maybe the leap from twelve to thirteen is like jumping over an Amazonian river, where you're not sure if you're going to make it or be eaten by piranhas instead. It was enough to make me want to hide under my pillow until I was out of this mess called "puberty."

Which, for the record, is the worst word *ever* in the history of all words.

Frowning, I plunked into my chair and turned

on my laptop. Darwin, who had been snoozing with his head under his wing, grumpily shuffled on his branch with his feathers ruffled.

It was time to take charge of my destiny.

Or in the very least, Google how to do it.

Hammering on my keyboard, all I had to do was type *how to get a guy to* and the autosuggestion came up: *how to get a guy to kiss you.*

Huh.

Maybe I wasn't the only clueless girl in the world, if so many people are wondering *how* exactly to get a guy to kiss you.

I scrolled through the links, clicking on the first web page. "Get a Guy to Kiss You in Three Easy Steps."

Bingo!

"This is it, Darwin!" I said, my excitement buzzing in my fingers.

I pored over the page eagerly. Maybe it really was this easy. A smile crept over my face as I pictured Kevin, dipping me in silhouette against a sunset for our first kiss with romantic accordion music playing in the background. But was it weird that I felt panicky? Even though it was just my imagination? That was totally normal, right?

Step 1: Look good. Wear something nice that plays up your very best features.

I stepped over to my closet, letting Darwin

shimmy up onto my shoulder. He clicked his beak in my ear as I inspected my clothes.

"Hmph," I said, poking at the mismatched tops that hung limply on their hangers. Clearly I would need to put some more thought into this part.

Step 2: Smell good. Boys don't want to be close to you if you smell like smoke, or body odor, or have bad breath. Make sure you have a breath mint.

I cringed. See, living in a zoo doesn't exactly do wonders for your smell. I shower and stuff, but the smell of animals in the air tends to sometimes… cling. I didn't reek like body odor or sweat, but what if I smelled like the sharks or something?

Ooh!

A light bulb went off in my head. I knelt on my floor and dug around under my bed, feeling for the cardboard box from Christmas. Mom had given me a spritzer of orange blossom body spray last year and I'd never found a good reason to try it out. What better reason than for your first kiss? I didn't even know oranges had blossoms, but maybe these body-spray gardeners knew something I didn't.

I stood in front of the mirror and spritzed some on my wrists where Keira Knightley does it in those perfume commercials. I took a quick sniff. It smelled like orangesicles, but it was still super faint. Maybe body spray wasn't as strong as real perfume?

Better give it a few more shots. And maybe one on my chest. When I was done spritzing, I definitely didn't smell like hippos.

Step 3: Ask him to teach you something. Boys love to feel useful, so giving them a chance to show off will make them like your company more. Now that you're bonding, when the moment is right, you'll know it! Lean in, close your eyes, and enjoy the moment!

Hmm.

I hadn't thought of that. Kevin was *always* teaching me things. He'd even tutored me for our math exam a couple months ago. Could he have wanted to kiss me then? Did this rule apply when the guy is supersmart and is basically always teaching *everyone*?

And what's this leaning in business? How much are you supposed to lean in? In the movies, the girl usually just has to lean in a teeny bit with her eyes closed, and the guy shoves his face toward her and they kiss all dreamy-like. Was I supposed to open my mouth? That's what the breath mint is for, right?

But what if I don't want to?

Can I kiss him and keep my lips closed? Or would that be too much like how I kiss my parents? What if Kevin thinks I'm a freak because I don't want to kiss him like *that*? Or does it even matter?! I bet he's not sitting there wondering this about *me*, so how much of a noob am I?!

Why is this so hard?!

"Time's a wastin'!" Darwin squawked in my ear. I shrugged him off to the top of his cage. He'd picked up that phrase from when Grandpa was here, always keen to start his next project.

"Okay, fine," I said, shoving my laptop away. "I'll call him." The fact that I knew this was inevitable didn't make the moment any easier. Like knowing you have to go to the dentist, but still not being able to stop the clammy-palm jitters while you're sitting there in the waiting room listening to those horrible drilling sounds.

I will call him. I will set up a real date and we will kiss and Liv won't leave me behind in the dust and we'll marry brothers and everything will be fine. Easy peasy.

Darwin chattered happily, scratching his head with his sharp claws. I wondered for a second if parrots made kiss pacts.

I picked up the phone and dialed Kevin's number before I could chicken out. I'd talked to him tons of times on the phone, so there was no reason to be scared, right? Just a first-kiss plan that he happened to not know about.

No big deal.

"Hello?" He answered on the second ring.

Ah, big deal!

"Uhhh," I stammered. I smacked the phone against my temple a couple times, trying to focus.

"Hello? Anyone there?" Kevin's voice was light, like he was close to laughing.

"Hi!" I yelled. Why did I always yell when I was nervous? "Hey, I mean," I said. "It's me. Ana. You know. *Annnaaaaahhh*."

Brilliant.

"I was wondering if you wanted to meet up some night?" I asked. I turned my back on Darwin, whose little beady eyes seemed to say, "You are such a fool."

But Kevin was normal Kevin. "Oh? You want to go to the robot shop with me and Daz?"

Gulp.

I hadn't thought that far ahead. What *were* we going to do? Besides, you know, hopefully kiss and not have me freak out about it.

"No!" I said. I dialed back the volume again. "No, I thought maybe you and I could go to…" I darted a look around my room, looking for inspiration. Dirty laundry? Nope. Darwin's dirty cage? Double nope.

A pile of unread books stared back at me from my desk. "The bookstore! I want to pick up a book and figured since you're supersmart there's probably *always* a book that you want to read, so…" I trailed off, hoping Kevin could fill in my obvious, spasmy gaps.

"Oh, cool!" he exclaimed. My breath rushed out

of me so loud he probably thought I was blowing up balloons over here. "That would be great. There's a couple new books I'd love to check out," he said.

I nodded, staring at my own widening eyes in my mirror. *Breathe.* "Cool. Okay then, so…how's Thursday? I can meet you at the zoo gate if your mom can give us a ride," I said. Thursday felt safe because I *knew* Friday was a date night thing, and I was afraid it would tip him off on my plan.

When I hung up the phone, I felt good. Like I could do anything. Maybe this whole growing up and being mature thing was more about faking it till you make it?

I stared at Darwin, who was bobbing his head like a maniac. "Ana banana! Closet banana!" he screeched.

I clapped my hand over my mouth. "That's right!. Step two! I need *clothes*!" I gawked at Darwin in a panic. He cocked his head and whistled ominously.

At least, I think it was ominous. Because the realization I had seemed to be accompanied with some pretty serious shock. There was only one person I could think of that would save me now.

"I need Ashley's help," I said.

"Ashley?" I ducked under the plastic tarp at the

Adventure Zone and headed straight for the locker room. A bellowy noise grew louder as I poked my head around the exhibit. "Hello? Anyone here?"

"Ana!" Patricia's voice was sharp. "Get in here right now!"

That didn't sound good. I raced to the back room.

"Patricia! What's the matter? Are you hurt?" I cracked open the door, bracing myself for whatever was on the other side.

But Patricia wasn't hurt.

Instead, she was surrounded by hermit crabs. And I don't mean in cages either.

"What the heck happened here?!" I leaped back from the door as crabs clicked their way underneath my feet. They were everywhere—under tank displays, creeping along near doorways, and skittering along the walls. Ashley was crouched on her knees, doing her best to scoop some of them up into a plastic bin. She glared at me with stony eyes.

Patricia's voice cut through me like glass. "I'll tell you what's happened," she said. She gestured through the window to the back of the crab exhibit. My eyes widened as I saw the lock, hanging limply on its hinge. The door had swung wide open, with sand and pebbles scattered all over the floor.

"Oh no!" I said. "How'd this happen?" I scratched my arms. Already the sight of them was making me itchy. I knelt down to help her gather them up one by one, trying to avoid the snippy little claws.

"Someone didn't lock the door before you left earlier. Ashley's got them cordoned off from the rest of the exhibit now, but we need to move fast. It was only you in here before." She held her hands on her hips. Her look of disappointment made my heart jolt. Behind her, Ashley was kneeling down beside a bucket, keeping her eyes on the swarming mass of crabs on the floor.

Panic washed over me. I *had* fed them earlier, before Ashley and I had started to sort shells. Had *I* done this?

Then I remembered the lock journal. Relief swirled through me. "I did feed them," I told her. "But I know I closed the lock, for sure. I wrote it in the journal too, like always."

She shook her head, the lines around her eyes softening. "Ana, you can tell me the truth."

"It is the truth!" I rushed over to the red notepad hanging by the fridge. "See. Right here." I pointed to today's date where I'd signed my name under the crab cage exhibit on the list. But when I looked down at the page, it was gone.

"Hey," I squeaked. This didn't make sense.

I examined the page, looking for smudges. I'd written it in the red wax pencil, exactly like every other time…

Patricia pursed her lips.

"Maybe you're remembering a couple days ago, Ana," Patricia said. She sounded defeated, like she wasn't going to believe me, no matter what I said. She replaced the notepad and wiped her sleeve across her forehead. "Come on. We need your help rounding these guys up."

"No!" I said. My voice was louder than I wanted it to be, but I *knew* I had double-checked that lock. *And* that I'd written my name in the journal.

Ashley's eyes darted to mine, then back to the ground in a flash. *Too* fast. Something was off.

Wait.

"It was Ashley!" I blurted. The words came tumbling out before I could stop them, but somehow *saying* them made me realize they were true. "She took my name off the list and undid the lock. I know it!"

Ashley's mouth dropped open. But this time I recognized her fake innocent face. I'd seen it a hundred times before when she'd been trying to ruin my life at school, where her head tilts just so and her eyes open extra wide. I'd also seen it the day of my big reptile presentation when she'd tried to mess that up for me too. There was no way I'd let her fool me this time.

My blood turned to ice.

I'd been so *stupid*.

Patricia swung around with fiery eyes. "Ana, that is a *very* serious accusation to make. Ashley has been a great help here, and I don't think that you have any right to accuse her," she said, punching every word like she meant it double. I stuck out my chin. There was no way Ashley would ruin this for me. Not this summer.

"But it's true!" The puzzle pieces snapped together in my mind, fitting together perfectly. I had to make Patricia understand. "She's been trying to sabotage me from the start! That's why those sea horses were overfed. She wanted me to get blamed for that too. And I *was*! She *hates* the zoo, and she's been trying to mess things up from the very beginning! I know it!"

Patricia's eyebrows shot up. "All right, Ana," she said. For a moment, I thought she was going to hear me out. Maybe she knew how Ashley had treated me in the past. But then her face darkened and she looked like my mom does in the store with Daz begging for video game money.

"I've got enough to worry about today. This place opens to the public this Saturday. I don't need any of this childish drama," she said. "Why don't you go home and take a break for a while?" She waved her hand in frustration. "Ashley and I can handle this. We're almost done anyway."

"What? You can't send me away," I said. Yelled,

really. Which I totally did not want to do, but why couldn't *anyone* see through Ashley's schemes? Meanwhile, Ashley was still staring at me like she was hoping I'd melt into the floor like a Popsicle.

"Thanks, Ana," she spat.

I started to fire back an insult, something—*anything* to stop Ashley from lying, but Patricia threw up her hands. "Enough! Ana, take the night and chill out. We can handle this."

She looked pointedly toward the door, just like Ashley and I had when we'd wanted Danielle to leave us alone a few hours earlier. Only now *I* was unwanted. "I think you should go home, Ana." She closed her eyes and took a deep breath, preparing herself to tackle the crabs again. Then she shoved through the door into the exhibit, leaving me standing there like a loser.

Top Five People You Should Never Ever Trust, No Matter How Much They Help You Find the Perfect Swimsuit

1. Ashley.
2. Ashley.
3. Ashley.
4. Ashley.
5. ~~The lady at Aviana's Bikini Hut~~ NOPE, JUST KIDDING. ASHLEY.

Chapter 15

Starfish are capable of regenerating missing limbs.

—Animal Wisdom

what about missing dignity? Can they regenerate that too? Because I sure could use some right about now.

I didn't go home straightaway. In fact, I didn't want to go home at all. I was sure that Patricia would tell my parents about what happened (even though it was completely one hundred percent untrue and sabotage), and I knew they would have that sinking look on their faces like the time I tried to steal a pack of Bubblicious watermelon gum from the store when I was seven.

But more than that, I was *mad*.

It was like all my insides were splintering apart, and it took all of my energy to hold myself together, instead of opening my mouth and *screaming* and letting all the pieces of me go flying out like shrapnel and hitting windows and innocent bystanders.

I wanted to get back at her. I wanted Ashley to feel as stupid as I did for thinking we could be friends. I wanted her to know I had figured it all out from the start, despite her little game of being nice to me and convincing me with swimsuits and mint chocolate chip ice cream. So I did what any girl who lives in a zoo would do when they were mad.

I hid in the crocodile pavilion.

Settling onto my favorite bench, I stared at Louis, the zoo's oldest crocodile. It was crazy to me that I'd been sitting right here a couple of months ago when a little girl named Beatrix asked me about crocodiles. Back then, I was worried Ashley would ruin my presentation.

Go figure that she was *still* being a monster to me now. Patricia's angry words kept repeating in my head, giving me a fresh rush of anger and shame to relive each time I played them back.

I whipped out my Anti-Ashley notebook and cracked the spine hard. Clearly her game had worked for a while, but I knew better now. Gripping a black pen in one hand, I began to scribble in dark, harsh letters. Louis watched me from his watery exhibit with dark, unreadable eyes.

TOP FIFTY REASONS ASHLEY IS THE WORST PERSON IN THE WORLD

A small bubble of satisfaction grew in my chest as I wrote. Too bad Ashley couldn't hear these in her head right now, wherever she was. *Then* she would know how horrible she was.

1. She acts so special and mature, but really she's only trying to make up for the fact that her sister, Rebecca, is, like, a zillion times prettier and better at everything.

2. Rayna and Brooke don't even like her. They're probably using her because Ashley was already popular when they got there, so Ashley is a free ride to being popular, without ANY work.

3. She's the most two-faced person on the planet. She will say anything to make herself look better, and then turn around and throw it in the other person's face like they don't matter AT ALL.

4. I bet no boys will ever truly like her. They'll think she's pretty and everything, but then when they get around her, they will learn she's horrible, and she will grow up bitter and have nobody who wants to kiss her...

I wrote and wrote and wrote. Eventually, my hand got cramped, but I kept writing anyway. People swarmed around me, knocking against my knees. But the words kept pouring out of me until I felt like I could breathe again. When I was finished, I had a scribbly mess that filled four pages. The pressure in my chest started to lighten as I leaned against the bench, focusing on the whir of the air around me and the chirping birds in the thick trees overhead.

Closing the notebook, I drummed my fingertips over the cover. It's funny how books seem to get heavier after you've written in them. Like the words you wrote somehow weighed more than the pages itself, holding all of your heavy emotions for you. I felt better after writing the list, but couldn't shake the feeling that the dark cloud over my head was now a rain cloud, pouring buckets of water all over me. What happened to my awesome summer?

I stuffed the notebook back into my bag and checked my watch. My parents would be worried if I wasn't home soon.

But of course I don't live in some movie where I can come home and have a heart-to-heart to figure out all of my problems. When I got home, the television was blaring a Shark Week program and the whole house smelled like burned popcorn.

Patricia hadn't called.

Nobody knew a thing.

A relieved, bleary numbness settled over me as I threw my backpack by the door and sank down next to Dad on the couch.

"Hey, Peanut. Where were you? I thought you finished earlier today? Bella called, by the way." He offered me the bowl of popcorn that was sitting beside him. The noises of Mom putzing around in the kitchen were loud above the sounds of thrashing great whites on the screen.

"Hey, Dad. Yeah, sorry. I went for a walk around the croc pavilion," I said, sinking down beside him. The sofa was so comfortable I wanted to sink into the cushions forever. Since when was summer so exhausting? "What's for dinner?"

Dad's lip curled slightly. "Your mom got some new recipe from Gail at work, but..." He looked forlornly toward the kitchen. "I really don't know," he said finally. The smell of something tangy snaked out of the kitchen toward us.

I smirked. I didn't mind that Mom wasn't a great cook. It meant we had lots of Michaelangelo's pizza, and how could you go wrong with that?

"Ooh, check that out!" Dad said suddenly, making me jump.

"What?" I blinked at the TV. A man in a life vest

was leaning over the edge of his boat, pointing at the massive shadow of a shark beneath the water. Then the camera flashed to the inside of a lab, where another guy in a white lab coat was peering through a microscope.

"New research," he explained. "They've discovered that some sharks live a lot longer than we thought."

"Huh," I said blankly. Snuggling back into the cushions, I let my eyes unfocus. I'd always thought sharks were cool, especially great white sharks. They seemed to swim around the ocean like they owned it. I shoved a handful of popcorn into my mouth. The buttery saltiness made me feel a teensy bit better.

"How come you think they're so good at it?" I asked aimlessly.

Dad thumbed the volume down on the controller. "Good at what?"

"You know," I said, picking a popcorn kernel from my teeth. "Good at being so *awesome* like that. They always seem so…in control." I watched in awe as a great white launched itself from the water, plowing into a seal like a freight train.

I mean, I felt bad for the seal and all, but still. I tried not to think about the little seal family that had been left behind after the great white turned him into dinner.

Dad sniffed. "It's true. They're basically the perfect predator. They've evolved to be great, I think. *Every* creature in the ocean knows better than to mess with them," he said with admiration. "They take charge, you know? Kick butt and take names!" His mustache wriggled.

A flicker of something stirred inside of me. Was that how I'd gone wrong with Ashley? Obviously I'd been dumb to even think we could be friends, but maybe I needed to take charge like a shark?

I mean, if I actually thought about it, that's pretty much what *Ashley* did, right? She'd gone and opened the lock and swiped my name off the journal to make it look extra bad for me. That was a *total* great white shark move. One hundred percent predator.

Maybe I needed to learn a lesson from Shark Week. You know how they say you have to fight fire with fire? Well, maybe the same went for fighting sharks. You had to *be* a shark to win it.

I toyed with the idea some more. "What about people taking charge like that?" I asked hesitantly. "You know, acting like a shark?" I waited for him to shake his head and tell me it was a horrible idea. But instead he raised his eyebrows.

"You know," he said, "there are probably worse animals you could be like. For example, you could be like a dung beetle and spend your life preoccupied with rolling in poop. Or you could be like a starfish and vomit up your own stomach every time you eat."

I made a face, squirming. "Ew, Dad," I said. "Now I can see where Daz gets it." I shoved him.

But despite Dad's poop/vomit talk, I knew I was onto something.

When Ashley started hanging out at the zoo, I'd tried to adapt, but really I'd been like a tiny fish, trying to avoid getting eaten by the big nasty shark, played by Ashley, of course. I did my best to keep her from messing me up, and for a while there, it *almost* looked like we could be friends. Well, not friends, but something *like* friends.

But after today? It was pretty obvious that it was all some big cruel joke so she could sabotage me at exactly the right moment.

I couldn't argue with Dad's shark logic. Being weak like prey had only worked for so long because Ashley is a Sneerer and I'd obviously forgotten about that. Now it was time to stop acting like a tiny fish.

It was time to act like an aggressive predator.

It was time to be a *shark*.

A couple hours later, I was towel drying my hair, enjoying the feeling of having washed that horrible day off my skin. I didn't have my perfect shark plan for Ashley yet, but I *had* gotten to have the longest bath in the world because Daz was out and wasn't around to pester me by knocking on the door and complaining that he needed the bathroom every ten minutes.

Of course, that didn't stop him from knocking on my bedroom door pretty much the second he got home.

No. Not knocking.

Pounding.

As in, he was *mad*.

"Where were you?" he demanded, storming into my room. He still had his shoes on and was carrying a tattered plastic bag. "I've called a bunch of times!"

"Excuse me?" I snipped, draping my hair towel over the end of my bed. "What are you yelling about?" Like I hadn't had a hard enough day without Daz getting on my case with his weirdness. "Go call Kevin if you need some subject for your robot experiments tonight," I said icily.

He dropped the bag on the floor with a thud. "Um, pretty sure I *would* if Kevin hadn't just spent the entire night helping out at an old-age home *selling Bella's cookies*!"

My heart screeched to a halt.

Bella.

The cookies.

Her bake sale!

"No!" I yelped. I collapsed onto my bed and held my head in my hands. "I didn't! I mean, I didn't mean to! *Oh noooo*," I wailed. "I totally forgot!"

He sat down beside me, with his shoulders drooping. "I tried to cover for you," he said grimly. His voice softened a notch. "But it was sort of hard since she knew you weren't busy tonight. Kevin said he tried calling, but that Dad said you weren't back yet."

I shook my head, swallowing down the guilt. "I feel terrible. I had such a bad day, and then—" I thought back to my spontaneous trip to the croc pavilion. I'd been writing an awful list about Ashley when I should have been setting up tables of cookies and bread for my *actual* friend.

"I got…distracted," I admitted. "Then when I got home I sort of zonked out on the couch with Dad."

He sighed. "Well, she's pretty upset."

I grimaced. I could practically see Bella's disappointed face already. She was always such a good friend to me, and I went and messed it up because I was too preoccupied with stupid Ashley.

"I'm such a jerk," I said. The truth hung in the air like a stinky dog towel on a rainy day. "I'll call her. I promise. Did she sell a lot?"

His frown turned to a devilish grin. "We did."

He stuck out his chest. "People even liked the sweet potato thingies," he said. "She was completely sold out. She saved these for you because she knew you liked them best." He nudged the container to me.

Relief rushed through me. At least she had done well. *Without my help at all.* I leaned against my pillow. It was Ashley's fault that I'd missed Bella's big night. I mean, *technically* it was me who forgot about it. But how could I not be distracted by her doing something so *awful*?

"Hey, Daz," I said, stretching over to kick my door closed.

"If I were to ask your help with something…" I ventured. "Would you do it?" I didn't know *what* I was thinking.

He raised his eyebrows. "You are not testing out makeup on me," he said, leaning away. "Or doing some weird dance routine…?"

I stared at him, dumbfounded. "What exactly do you think girls *do* all day? Put on makeup and choreograph dances? Please."

He shrugged. "I only know what I see in the movies," he admitted, narrowing his eyes. "Who *knows* with you people?"

I went on, keeping my voice low. "I know you're good at…secret stuff," I said. "I may need your help later, that's all."

If I ever thought of the perfect sharky plan, that is.

"Do you want to rob a bank?" he asked, sighing dejectedly. "I already promised Mom I wouldn't break the law," he whined. "I mean, all that money is probably just *sitting there*." He raised his fists to the ceiling.

"Whoa," I said, grabbing his arm. "Calm down. It's not illegal. I'm having a problem with someone, that's all."

He puffed up again. "A problem? Need me to beat someone up? That's what big brothers are for!" He stood up, tripping over the sheet. "*Let me at him!*"

Sometimes I think he really might be adopted.

"You're not my big brother, Daz. I'm four minutes older than *you*," I pointed out.

He sniffed. "Yeah, but I'm taller. So…*bigger*."

"I'll let you know what I decide," I said. He nodded and slunk back to his room.

Something must be wrong with me. Was I seriously considering getting Daz's help with Ashley? I looked at the small container of no-bake cookies Daz had brought me. I *hated* letting Bella down. And it wouldn't have happened without Ashley being such a sabotaging jerk. Whoever said girls just want to have fun was a total lame-o. The truth? Girls just want to survive until high school.

Chapter 16

The common octopus can eject a cloud of black ink to hide itself from predators.

—Animal Wisdom

If humans had that ability, I'm pretty sure I'd spent 98 percent of my life covered in black ink. Just saying.

I called Bella first thing the next morning to beg for her forgiveness. I promised her I'd be her recipe tester until the end of time, even for the scary-looking cookies with weird seeds that didn't have any sugar in them. It was the least I could do, considering how much of a turd I'd been.

She wasn't angry at me, at least not nearly as

angry as she should have been. Somehow that made me feel even guiltier. Here I was worried about stupid Ashley, while everyone else seemed to be having loads of fun and making cookies and having normal summer fun.

I didn't have time to figure out a perfect revenge plan for Ashley yet. But I *did* get an e-mail from Liv during the night.

And on the list of things Ana Wasn't Ready For, it was sitting near the top.

Dear Ana,

I've been doing some thinking about our kissing pact, and I think I have an idea! You know that saying, "Luck favors the prepared mind," right? Ms. Harris had a poster of it in our English class last year. Anyway, I was thinking, this could be the key for us! We have to prepare for our first kiss! I think to get ready we should do the thing we've been talking about doing for six months now. Let's have a leg shaving day! We can shave our legs together and that will show the universe that we're READY to be women! Real women with shaved legs and lipstick and dates! Our first kiss is bound to follow, right? What says "kiss me" like super-smooth legs like those girls on the shaving cream commercial? I bet they get kissed all the time! Plus, this is perfect timing because I'm going out with Leilani this weekend to see a movie and she's bringing this cute guy, Ryan, and I'm wearing an adorable dress and don't want him to think I'm some little kid with hairy legs!

I'll chat with you online tomorrow at exactly 4 p.m., your time. Be ready!

—Liviola xoxoxo

Ugh.

Now, *somehow* I was sitting in my computer chair with a bottle of Nair beside me, waiting for Liv to ding me so we could start our video chat. And believe me, I was S-C-A-R-E-D. I could imagine every single hair on my leg staring up at me, pleading, "Why do you want to cut us all off, Ana?!"

I know.

I'm such a wuss.

But I would seriously rather wrangle an angry crocodile than shave my legs. Razors are freaky! Did you know that the razors in the commercials are supersharp, like a *surgeon's* knife! I don't want a surgeon's knife going anywhere near my legs! One blade is bad enough, but I checked and Mom's razor has *five* all lined up like some demented grin with five rows of teeth. What if I impale myself and have to go to the hospital and end up with a limp or something? Can you imagine what Ashley or the other Sneerers would say? What if I had to have my whole leg amputated?

Plus, once you started shaving your legs, you couldn't quit. I've seen Mom's legs when she goes a few days without shaving hers and believe me it is not pretty. It's like she's part porcupine!

But I decided that Liv was right. If shaving my legs (or Nairing them in my case because heck no to the razors) was going to get me a kiss, then it had to be worth it. I mean, maybe Nairing my legs was what a shark would do too, and therefore the perfect "take charge" idea?

Even though it was terrifying.

Diiiiiinnnnnggggg!

I scrambled for my computer mouse, clicking the "Receive Call" button. Liv's face appeared on the monitor. She was in her bathroom, with her laptop propped up on the sink. Her hair was wrapped up in a towel.

"Hey!" she squealed. "Are you ready? Why aren't you in the bathroom? You're not bailing on me, are you? This is the perfect plan!"

I shook my head. "No, I'm not bailing," I reassured her. I didn't tell her how freaked I was about razors. Or about losing my leg hair in general. "I'm going to use Nair," I said. "It's supposed to last longer than shaving, and that way I don't have to use up bathroom time until it's time to wash it off. Daz won't be able to bug me in here," I said. Everything in my explanation sounded reasonable. I tried to channel my bravest, sharkiest thoughts.

"Oh, gotcha," she said. "So you want to go at the same time?" Her eyes glimmered with excitement. "I'm so glad we're doing this. Leilani said she started shaving her legs when she was *ten*!" She grabbed the can of shaving cream beside her and squirted some into her palm.

"Ew, why?" I asked, wishing I could take the words back the moment they popped out. I tried not to show Liv how much Leilani annoyed me. Especially considering I had never even *met* her. But still.

She shrugged. "Okay, you go too," she said, once her leg was lathered up. "This way I can shave while you're waiting for the Nair. How long are you supposed to leave it on?"

I shook the tube and read the label. "It says five to seven minutes," I said. "Here goes nothing." I opened the tube and leaned over in my chair, running a thick line up my shin. "It's *cold*," I muttered.

"Does it smell good? Maybe I'll use some next time," Liv said.

I took a whiff. "Oof." My stomach lurched. "It smells like rotting plants! Gross!" Liv giggled as I spread the lotion around on my leg. It was like icing a stinky leg cake. Already my skin was beginning to tingle. As I did, Liv ran the razor from her ankle to her kneecap.

"This feels weird," she said. "Like tugging on my leg. I think it's working though!" She grinned to me, showing off the missing strip of shaving cream.

I smiled back. Maybe this was okay, the whole shaving thing. Maybe some things should happen whether you were ready for them or not, you know? I wiped the leftover Nair from my hands and set the timer on my computer to ding in exactly five minutes. The tingling on my skin was getting more intense, so it must be working. My hairs were probably dissolving magically under all that goo.

"So…" I ventured. "Do you have a plan for your first kiss yet?" I asked. I didn't tell her that I'd planned an almost-date with Kevin, because I still had hopes I could forget the whole kiss part of it.

When we were younger, we had a pact to eat only things that started with the letter *b*. And like the kiss pact, it was her idea. She lasted two days, and after eating about a zillion bananas, broccoli, and bread, she decided it was a dumb idea. All I had to do was wait it out. Maybe this kiss pact would be the same?

If she hadn't had any luck so far, this could be the perfect way out of our pact without me looking like a little kid.

"Yes!" she squealed.

My heart fell as she dipped her razor in the water and took another swipe. "His name is Ryan! He's one of Leilani's friends, and ever since I moved here, he's been super nice to me." She sighed dreamily. "We're all going to the movies next weekend, so I'm thinking maybe then! It's dark and cozy in those theaters, you know?"

I frowned at my legs. The tingling was getting worse now. I imagined all the tiny hairs, slowly meeting their demise. I wasn't surprised Liv had already met a cute guy, but how could she want to kiss him *already*? I'd known Kevin for *years* and I still didn't feel brave enough to kiss him.

"How about you?" She shaved another clean line up her leg with the razor. "What's the plan for Kevin?"

I peered at the timer on my screen, cringing when I saw I still had three minutes left. This was starting to *hurt*.

"What's the matter?" Liv asked. She moved closer to the screen, inspecting me from a zillion miles away. "You look like you ate some bad eggs!"

I winced. "I think..." I said, leaning down close

to my legs. The smell was awful, but that wasn't my only problem. "I think something's wrong with the Nair." What started as tingling had now morphed into *burning*.

Like fire.

On the surface of the sun.

"Is burning normal? Should it hurt? Ahh, it's *really* stinging now!" I panicked, zipping around my room, trying to get some cool air onto my legs. "*Oww!*"

"I don't know! Maybe you should wipe some off and see!" Liv's eyes were wide. She was still gripping her razor but didn't budge from the screen.

I scrambled for the cool, damp towel that I'd stolen from the bathroom earlier. Swiping at my knee, I felt an instant blast of coolness.

"Oh God, what is *that*?" Liv screeched.

I stared down at my knee. "No, no, no!" I said. The dread in my stomach mixed with the smell of the Nair threatened to make me puke. Angry red bumps stared back at me, covering the entire section of my leg that I'd cleaned off.

I was hairless, all right. But now I was also a *leper*.

"Go take it off! Now, Ana!" Liv yelled. "With water!"

"I gotta go!" I said between clenched teeth. I didn't want to seem like a giant baby here, but *wow this hurt.* I beelined for the bathroom and hopped in the tub, turning on the cold water. And because the world can't give me one single, stupid break, Daz burst in the room.

"Hey! I was just coming in here. I have to pee!" He paused, taking in the sight of me standing in the tub in my shorts, frantically clawing at my legs, and the angry, red welts that were sprouting all over them.

"What's all that? Ooh, dude, that looks like a horror movie!" He leaned in excitedly and swiped at some of the Nair on the towel with his fingertip. He sniffed it. "Gah! What is this?! It smells like zombies!"

"Get out of here!" I yelled, then clutched at his shirt sleeve. "Is Mom home?!" I could feel hot tears streaming down my face. It hurt too much to care about. I twisted the faucet to even colder water.

Daz scratched his head, looking worried. "No, she's with the lions. Do you want me to call an ambulance?" His face was serious.

"No!" I screamed. "I don't know! It *kills*!"

Daz dashed from the room, returning a couple minutes later with Dad in tow. "Don't worry! I got Dad!"

"Okay, sweetheart," Dad said. He gripped under my armpits with his hands. "Let's get you out of here so I can check you over," Dad said, pulling me toward him. I couldn't remember the last time I wanted my parents so bad.

So much for being tough and taking charge of my life.

I bet there have been zero sharks in history that needed their fathers to save them from Nair attacks.

It took a few minutes to calm me down, but once Dad gave me one of the antiallergy pills from the medicine cabinet, the burning began to calm down.

"You had an allergic reaction," Dad explained. He handed me a glass of cold lemonade. "Did you talk to your mother about using Nair on your legs? I think she's allergic too," he said.

Well, *that* information might have been nice before I slathered it all over myself.

I shook my head. "Liv and I wanted to do it together," I said. I didn't tell him about our kiss pact (hello, he's my *dad* and how embarrassing would that be?), but I did tell him that it was Liv's idea and that I was simply trying to avoid using his razor, which was sort of a white lie, but partly true, right?

"Ana," he said sternly. "I know she's your best friend. But what works for her might not always work for you, and that's okay. And next time, talk to your mother or me if you want to try some weird product." He sniffed the air. "That stuff *stinks*, kiddo."

I swallowed hard. Sometimes I didn't get parents. Usually, Mom and Dad are always going on about me doing things that I'm afraid of, like presenting in front of people and trying to eat artichokes for the first time. They say it's *good* to do things that you aren't ready for, right? It meant you were brave or fighting against your fears.

Or something.

Now I was getting lectured to not try new things without running it by them? Couldn't they make up their minds?

"On the upside," Dad said, his face breaking into a smile, "at least we know Daz isn't allergic."

"Huh?" he asked, plunking down beside us with his own lemonade. A strip of his eyebrow, right at the edge of his left eye, was missing.

Dad wrapped his arm around Daz, who squirmed under the weight. "Did you touch some of the Nair, Daz? And then touch your face perhaps?" His shoulders shook with laughter.

I giggled as Daz checked out his reflection in the toaster. A smear of Nair was still streaked by his temple, beside the missing half of his eyebrow.

"Aww, *man*," he said, wiping the cream with his sleeve.

"You look like a Picasso painting!" I yelled, pointing at him. "Bahahaha!" I toppled over beside

Dad. Okay, so the allergic reaction totally sucked, but Daz losing his eyebrow? Pretty much made this whole thing worth it.

"Wait till your mother hears this one," Dad said, and shook his head with fake pity.

Chapter 17

Great white sharks can sense electric fields.
—*Animal Wisdom*

Can they sense people who lie through their teeth and pretend to be your friend by helping you shop for swimsuits? Didn't think so.

They say traumatic situations can give you a whole new perspective.

That's partly true, because after that whole Nair experience, you wouldn't catch me within ten feet of that evil goop again. But the part that *didn't* change about my perspective was how much I wanted to get back at Ashley. Somehow, the fiery welts on my legs had made me even angrier.

I needed to dig deep. Put on my big girl panties and all that.

So the next day, armed with a fresh set of *almost* spot free legs, I showed up to the Adventure Zone. But now things would be different. I wasn't going to kid myself this time. Ashley was a jerk. She was a two-faced pretender who tricked me, and though I felt ridiculously stupid about it, I would hold my head high and be the bigger man.

Woman.

Whatever.

And my number-one priority? I would think of the *perfect* revenge.

Ashley was organizing a display of shark jaws when I stepped beyond the tarp.

She looked up. "Hey," she said softly.

Seriously? After she sabotages me, she has the guts to say hello?

No. I told myself. Don't fall for it again. Ashley is not your friend. She's probably worried about looking bad in front of Patricia, now that I know the truth.

Instead of responding, I glared at her. Let her see what it feels like. I even tried to raise my eyebrows in that super-haughty way that I'd seen her use at school.

"Ana," Patricia said. "Welcome back." She reached out and squeezed my shoulder. She was trying to be extra nice, but I didn't want to think about it. Not now, when I was doing my best to give Ashley the cold shoulder.

"I'm glad you're here," she said. "Logan is gone for the day, and I need you guys to prepare for Saturday's grand opening. We need to have this place completely cleaned and tidied, okay? Ashley can do floors, and you can clean the tank windows."

"Okay," I said. I didn't mean for my voice to sound so cold, but could she blame me? I couldn't help but notice that all around me, scary creatures were circling. Ashley outside the tanks, and sharks inside them.

I ignored Ashley as I set off to the back room to collect the cleaning supplies. For the next half hour, I spritzed all of the tanks with cleaner, wiping them down with paper towels. The silence in the room spread out around us like a storm cloud, angry with rain and ready to burst.

I didn't hear Ashley approach me at the sea dragon tanks. "How's it going?" she asked. Her voice was low and hesitant.

I gave her my best "I'm above this conversation" look. "What does it matter to you?" I said coldly. Ugh, I was so bad at this. Already I felt guilty and jerky and stupid all wrapped up into a ball of mean. But I couldn't give in. She had proven who she was.

Be the shark.

Her face morphed into an angry mask. "What's your problem, Ana?! I thought we could forget about all this and get back to normal, okay? Is that so wrong? Why are you being such a pill?!" She crossed her arms over her chest.

I snorted. "Oh, sure. Just forget that you're a total jerk and you tricked me into actually *liking* you for a moment. Not gonna happen, sorry." My face burned so hot I was afraid the water around me would start steaming.

Her mouth tipped down at the corners, and her eyes narrowed. "I told you I didn't do anything. *You* were the one who'se name wasn't on that journal! And I wasn't *tricking* you! Thanks for telling Patricia I did it! *I'm* the one who should be angry at *you*!"

I rolled my eyes. "Yep. My name randomly decided to wipe itself off, and that cage magically opened by itself." I stood up from the tank. "You were the *only* person here, Ashley! It's not like I would sabotage *myself*."

The air was cool around us, but it felt thick and sticky, like tar, to me. Like I was stuck in a pool of messed-up feelings and couldn't get out. "Look. I promised I'd help you with your presentation, and I'm not a lying jerk, so I will, if you want. But that's it." I kept my voice hard.

She sniffed, but her face turned icy. It was like watching a switch go off inside her head. One moment, she was angry. The next, like she was a robot. How did someone get so good at turning off their emotions like that?

"I don't need any more help," she spat. "I made flash cards from everything to study, and Patricia told me I could use my notebook if anyone has questions that stump me. So I will," she said simply. She clutched the blue notebook I had given her to her chest. A dark flicker of amusement blipped inside of me when I thought about my *own* blue notebook and how it was filled with every mean thing about Ashley that I could think of.

"Fine," I said.

Ugh. I *hate* the word *fine*. It means anything *but* fine and everyone knows it. But I didn't care.

"I don't know why you're being so immature here." Ashley's lip curled in disgust. "I didn't *do* anything. You're the one being a whiner about everything."

A *whiner*?!

My insides felt like they were cracking at the seams. I glared at the notebook in her arms, wanting to grab it from her and rip it to tiny pieces. I bet she wouldn't feel so confident if she didn't have her precious *notes*.

That's when the idea hit me.

It wasn't nice.

It wasn't like *me* at all.

But it was definitely a *shark* idea, and that had to be a good thing.

Memories of my first crocodile presentation came flooding back. The snarky look on Ashley's face when she was hoping *so badly* for me to mess up. The way she tried to film the whole thing, so she could put it on the Internet for future generations to see how much of a loser I was.

The idea wrapped around my heart like a boa constrictor, squeezing me desperately. She'd tried to ruin my presentation.

So maybe my perfect sharky plan would be to ruin *hers*.

No, I wasn't going to cause a scene and make her forget her notes or anything. That would probably end up with *me* looking stupid somehow. Instead, I could *switch* my notebook for hers.

It was obvious she was nervous and would need her notes, right? So instead of opening her notebook and seeing shark notes when she needed them, she would see *all* the reasons she was a total backstabbing jerk to me.

It was simple.

It was brilliant.

I just needed some help to get it done.

"Good luck," I said sharply.
I knew what I needed to do.

Later that night, I left a note in Daz's room, tapped to the side of Oscar's tank.

Daz,
It's me. Remember how I said I might need your help with something? Meet me by the scorpions in the Americas Pavilion at 4:30 tomorrow afternoon. I'll explain everything then.

—A

P.S. Burn this letter. No wait, don't do that. You'll probably set the house on fire and Mom will freak. But seriously, tear it up and eat it or something. This is top-secret business.

Chapter 18

Cuttlefish can blend seamlessly into their
surroundings by changing color.
—*Animal Wisdom*

Think like a cuttlefish. Think like a cuttlefish.

So it turns out that being a criminal is a lot more
nerve-racking than it sounds.

The next day, I waited until our work was almost
done and excused myself early, with my stomach
performing Cirque du Soleil's latest acrobatic
routine. Ashley didn't bat an eyelash, and Patricia
was so busy getting ready for the opening tomorrow that she barely knew we were even there in
the first place.

Nobody knew that I didn't really have a stomachache. Nobody saw me double back around the exhibit and sneak over to the Americas Pavilion. The scorpion exhibit was dark, with glow-in-the-dark posters of bugs all around. It was the perfect place to hatch my plan without anyone hearing.

Ducking inside, I settled against the wall and checked my watch.

4:28 p.m. Don't fail me now, Daz.

But he poked his head out from around the scorpion tank right on time.

"*Psst!*" he hissed into the darkness.

"I'm right here, Daz," I said. "You don't need to whisper. What the heck is that on your head?" I looked quizzically at the old-timey brimmed hat.

Daz grinned. "Your note said this was top-secret business! This is my secret agent hat."

"You look like you're a gangster," I said. "And a grubby one at that." I swiped away one of Darwin's feathers from the brim, sending it floating to the ground.

"I could be both," he said. Sitting down next to me on the bench, he peered around us in the dark. We were alone. "So. What's up? It sounds important."

"I need your help," I said. For a moment, I was surprised to hear those words coming out of my mouth. You *know* I'm in a pickle if I'm asking Daz for his opinion.

"Ashley's being a giant pain, and I want to teach her a lesson." My heart began to race in my chest. This all felt so…so *criminal*.

I clenched my fists. *Stop it. Sharks don't feel guilty.*

His eyes widened. "Seriously? That doesn't sound like you." He frowned. "What did you want to do?"

I drummed my fingers on my knee. "Nothing too serious," I said. "I don't want to *hurt* her or anything. I was thinking about…her notebook," I said.

Daz didn't react. "What notebook?"

"There's a notebook she has that she's been keeping all her notes in for our shark stuff. Since she's giving a presentation at the opening, I thought that maybe—" I paused. This didn't feel right. I swallowed hard, shoving the thought away. Ashley's sneering face flickered in my mind, reigniting my anger. "I was thinking it would be awfully hard for her to remember everything without her notebook," I said finally. The words rushed out, leaving a twisted feeling deep in my stomach. "So I'm going to switch it," I said. "With an *empty* one." I kept my eyes down, in case Daz could tell I was lying on that one.

Daz leaned back against the bench, tapping his face with his fingertip. I did the same thing when I was thinking hard. "Are you serious? That's like… pretty mean," he said finally.

I huffed. "Well! She sabotaged me! She left the

locks open to make it look like I did, and—and," I stammered. "What else am I supposed to do?! Will you help me or not?!" The prick of tears behind my eyes made me turn away. I was *not* going to cry in front of Daz. Not in a zillion years would I live that down.

"I'll help you!" he said, holding out his hands in apology. "Did you want me to switch her notebook? Or do you want me to show you how to do it yourself?"

Relief swelled through me. "You'll help me." I breathed, nodding to myself. "Okay."

"Well, duh. I am your brother." He smirked. "Besides, you'll have a much better chance of not getting *caught* with my help," he said.

I laughed. "I don't know if being a criminal genius is something you should be proud of," I pointed out.

"Comes in handy now though, doesn't it?" Daz beamed.

"Just tell me what to do." I glanced at my watch again. "I want to get this done tonight. She'll leave her notebook in her locker and take her flash cards home to study. I need help with the locker."

Daz nodded. "You might want to write this down," he said sneakily. "Daz action plans are *always* meticulous."

Meticulous?

"Have you been reading Dad's word-a-day calendar again?" I rolled my eyes at the look he shot me. "Okay! Okay! Officially writing down. Go ahead." I dug into my backpack and pulled out a pen, poising it over the back of an Adventure Zone pamphlet. "What's the first step?"

Daz glanced around us to make sure we were still alone. "'Kay. Here's what you need to do."

The sharp yelp of a zoo visitor outside made me nearly jump out of my skin.

"Breathe," I told myself. "You can do this."

I leaned against the Adventure Zone wall, peeking inside the back room. Nobody knew I was in here. Daz's plan was foolproof, but apparently it wasn't "Ana-proof," because I'd already stubbed my toe trying to be all *Mission: Impossible*–like against the walls. Ashley was putting her stuff in her locker, humming to herself. Logan was in the cafeteria with Danielle, eating curly fries. Patricia was helping someone in the polar bear exhibit.

For the record, it's super weird watching someone when they think you're not there anymore, and it made me feel like a total creeper. But I couldn't avoid it.

This is my only shot.

I ran through Daz's plan in my head one more time. All I had to do was wait for Ashley to change her shirt, like she did every day right before she left. After watching her a zillion times, I knew she always grabbed it from her bag, threw it over her shoulder, and ducked into the bathroom to wash up and change. She always left her locker open to do it.

At least, she *better* today, because this whole revenge thing depended on it.

I would sneak in, switch the notebook in her locker for mine, and bolt.

Easy as revenge pie.

I tried to steady my breathing, timing it with the drone of the filters all around me. Was it just me or were they quieter today? Why did I feel about a thousand times louder than normal? Could the sharks tell I was up to no good? Is this the kind of paranoia criminals live with all the time?

I ducked as Ashley grabbed her backpack and threw it on the bench. From here, she looked normal again. Almost nice. There was no snarky anger in her eyes. She riffled through her things, pulling out a green shirt. Daz's instructions recited in my head.

Step one. Get inside the room without her hearing you.

I held my breath as she swung the shirt over her shoulder. Yes! This was working! She crossed the room and went into the bathroom. Her locker was still open.

I could do this.

I am stealthy like James Bond.

Leaning into the door, I let it open slowly. No loud squeaks or creaks here. I slipped in the room carefully, checking the floor for anything that I, Captain Clumsy, could possibly trip on. So far, so good.

I waited a moment, staring at the bathroom door. I could faintly hear Ashley humming behind it, and then the water started running. I froze; my hand was suspended in midair, reaching toward her locker. The notebook was sitting there on the top shelf, practically daring me.

Step two. Switch the notebooks as quickly as possible. Do not let anything fall to the floor or it might tip her off that you were there.

Gingerly, I pulled out the notebook, making sure none of the other papers or books tumbled out after it. I flipped it open, making sure it was the right book. Drawings of seashells stared back at me. She had made notes after our shell sorting day. I touched a small drawing of a murex shell. It was the shell she had taken home with her. Small ballpoint pen stars surrounded it.

I swallowed hard as my stomach clenched with doubt.

No. None of that mattered now.

The water in the bathroom stopped running. She could come out any second.

I sucked in a breath.

Step three: Get out way before you have to, so there's no chance of her seeing you leave the exhibit.

Ashley sneezed from inside the bathroom, jerking me back into action. It was too late. She couldn't find me going through her stuff. I tucked the notebook under my arm, shoved mine in its place, and bolted back through the door, leaving her locker open the way it was when I'd arrived.

The door thumped closed behind me.

Outside the air was thick and hot. Visitors bustled around me as I hid the book as best I could by my side and hustled away from the Adventure Zone. The word *criminal* seemed to echo through me as my sandals slapped the hard pavement. I forced myself to slow down and walk like a normal person.

Nobody knew anything. I'd done it. When it came time for Ashley to present, she would have to do it *without* her handy notes. And as a bonus, she would see all the ways she'd been horrible to me in their place.

It was only fair, I told myself, considering how much of a jerk she'd been to me.

Once I made it home, I bolted for my room and

shoved her notebook under my bed as Darwin glared at me with glittering black eyes. He clicked his beak in disgust. At least I think it was disgust because I felt pretty disgusting.

"What?" I snapped. "All I'm doing is teaching her a little lesson," I hissed. "She tried to ruin my presentation too!"

He fluttered his wings and turned away from me.

"Oh, come on," I said. "She might not even *need* her stupid notes, with all the memorizing she's been doing," I rationalized. It was true. Ashley *had* been working hard to get her presentation right; she would probably coast through perfectly fine. It's not like she'd be worried about *me* if the situation were reversed, right?

I faced myself in the mirror and wiped at a line of sweat that was forming on my forehead, despite the air-conditioned house.

This didn't feel the way I thought it would. I closed my curtains, throwing an inky darkness over my room. I didn't want to hear the lions roaring or the zoo visitors chatting. Curling up in bed, I closed my eyes.

I knew I'd done the right thing.

So why did I feel so…*wrong*?

Chapter 19

Dolphins use echolocation to track their prey, making up to one thousand clicking noises per second.

—Animal Wisdom

I wonder how the FBI track criminals? They probably have better systems than dolphins, that's for sure.

I am not going to jail.

I am not going to jail.

I am not going to—*wait*—what was that noise?!

I whirled around in my chair at the loud creak outside my door, sending Darwin scuttling from my desk to his open cage.

"Shh!" I hushed his indignant chirps.

Could that be the cops?!

It had been a few hours since I'd switched Ashley's notebook, and it seemed like any second the police would be here, pounding on the door and ready to haul me into jail. I mean, they probably had much scarier criminals to catch than some notebook stealer. But who knows, right? They could be having a slow night.

All through dinner I'd been a jumpy mess, and I even got chicken wing sauce on Dad because I'd dropped the takeout box onto his foot. How did criminals live with the fear? All I knew was, I was *not* going to leave my room unless it was for a very good reason.

Too bad I'd totally forgotten about what should have been the best reason of all.

I recoiled at another creak outside my door, followed by a light knock.

"Hey, Ana?" For a moment, I thought it was Daz, but then I realized that Daz has never knocked *or* been quiet for a moment in his life.

"Are you there? Did you still want to go to the bookstore?"

The bookstore?

The *bookstore*! My heart dropped to my stomach.

Kevin!

I'd totally forgotten our date! Was it Thursday already?

"What is *wrong* with me?" I whisper-hissed and glared at Darwin as I bolted out of my chair to my closet, knocking over my lemonade onto my lap in the process. He *couldn't* know I forgot. Yanking through the hangers, I searched for something to wear. Of course, now after the whole Ashley thing, I had zero fashion ideas. Teal shirt and khaki shorts? Black tank and jeans? Who forgets a date with the cutest super-genius guy ever?! *Where is my body spray?!*

"*Braack! What's wrong with me?*" Darwin crowed. I pelted a dirty sock at his head.

Another knock. "Uh…you okay in there? I can come back…" Kevin said. Then Mom's voice echoed through the house.

"Ana! Are you in there? Kevin is here!"

Thanks for the warning, Mom.

I pulled open my door, trying not to look like a complete lunatic. The lemonade stain on my shorts was cold and sticky against my leg.

Be cool, Ana.

"Hey!" I shouted, trying to act like I was sane and hadn't forgotten about him. I looked back at Darwin, who was nuzzling the backup shirt I'd chosen. Getting his feathery face all over it. "Um." I held out my finger. "Just one sec. I need to change. I smell like hippos! Go hang out with my parents, and I'll be right there!" I said frantically.

Super smooth, Ana.

Kevin laughed and turned back to the kitchen as I slammed the door closed.

What were the kissing tips again?

I pulled my shirt over my head, switching to a cleaner one. At this point, if it didn't have a lemonade stain or smell like a barnyard, I was ahead of the game. Standing tall, I checked myself out in the mirror, hoping that I looked mature and sophisticated and kissable and all those things that girls on the magazines look like.

Instead I looked like I'd just run a marathon. *Argh*.

I *so* did not feel like I was first-kiss ready in this outfit. Did all first almost-dates feel so rushed? My hair was in a messy ponytail, and my cheeks were beet red. Probably from being scared out of my wits that it was the FBI at the door looking for Ashley's stolen notebook, instead of Kevin.

No! Don't think about that now!

I sniffed my shirt. I still smelled like guilty sweat. Digging around under a pile of clothes on my floor, I still couldn't find my body spray. Tiptoeing across the hall, I ducked into my parents' bedroom. Mom always had perfume lying around on the top of her dresser. I grabbed a curvy blue bottle from the little tray and spritzed some in the air, running through the mist.

Wait.

Sniffing the air, I realized my mistake. Mom usually smells like vanilla and toasted marshmallows or fresh, breezy oceans.

I didn't smell like Mom. I smelled like Dad.

I smelled like a boy.

Dad had put his cologne on Mom's side of the dresser.

"*Noooo.*" I breathed, sinking onto their bed. "No, no, no, no, no." I sniffed the collar of my shirt, testing the smell. Maybe it wasn't that strong? My nose curled in disgust. I *couldn't* show up on my first ever almost-date and smell like a boy. Why was I so bad at this?! Was this bad karma for the Ashley-notebook thing?

I eyed the other bottles. The blue bottle smelled like woodsy boy, but maybe there was a perfume of Mom's that would…complement it? What goes with the woods?

Lifting the bottles, I took a whiff of each one. The mix of my dad's cologne and mom's perfume made my head spin, but I finally decided upon the marshmallowy perfume. I mean, woods and marshmallows go together, right? Where else are you supposed to cook s'mores? Smelling like a nice campfire treat in the woods can't be a *bad* thing.

I prayed to the almost-date gods as I sprayed myself with Mom's bottle. Too bad my nose was too fried to tell if it did any good. I gave one final spritz in the air, walking through the mist on my way out the door.

In the living room, Mom was all smiles. And I don't mean normal smiles. I mean the "I-know-what-you're-up-to-young-lady-and-I-can't-believe-my-little-girl-is-growing-up-it's-killing-me-to-not-get-the-camera-out" smiles. Dad was beside her on the couch, flipping through a thick wad of papers for work. "Kevin said you two are heading to the bookstore?" Mom cooed, giving me the quickest wink in history.

I nodded brusquely, eyeing Kevin to make sure he hadn't seen it. Luckily he's a boy and misses pretty much everything involving daughter-mother interactions. "Yep. We don't need a ride," I said. "Kev's mom is going to take us."

Dad looked up, sniffing the air. "Anyone smell that?"

I cleared my throat. This could not be happening. "Okay! We're outta here!" I mumbled, grabbing Kevin by the arm and heading for the door.

"Have fun, you two!" Mom called out, giggling.

Cue eternal embarrassment.

The bookstore smelled like coffee and cookies.

This *would* have been an awesome thing because usually I like the smell of cookies and coffee. But this time all it did was clear my head and nose enough to notice something: I smelled.

No.

Smelled isn't the right word.

I *reeked*.

It took me about three minutes in the store to notice that my perfume mess combo was probably the worst idea I'd ever had. Worse than the time I tried to dye my hair with Magic Markers when I was six. And worse than the time I tried to hide my hamster, Sir HamstaLot, in my closet when I was five years old because I was *convinced* he was only "playing dead."

No wonder Kevin's mom kept sneezing in the car.

Kevin strolled through the aisles, looking for his usual section in science and technology. I tried to keep a safe distance, hoping that the smell wouldn't get to him. What sucked even more is that if you're out to get your first kiss, keeping your *distance* isn't exactly the best plan.

But I wasn't going to be defeated. Not by some marshmallow-rotten-woods smell at least. After chomping on three breath mints until my eyes started watering, I decided to move on to step three and get Kevin to teach me something so he could feel important and special.

"So can you tell me about this?" I smiled as flirtatiously as I could and pulled out a book from the shelf.

The mints were still making my eyes blurry, so I couldn't exactly *see* what book I picked. Kevin's eyebrows lifted in surprise.

"*Nature's Most Dangerous Parasites*," he read, frowning. "You want me to tell you about parasites?"

I shoved the book back on the shelf, trying to hide my dismay with a well-timed cough. Parasites are like the least kissable thing on the planet. I wiped my eyes. The perfume-mint combo was really getting to me now.

"Um, I meant this one," I said, grabbing another title. "*Biomimicry*," I said. A rush of relief swept through me. That was safe enough. No disgusting parasites to ruin the mood there.

Kevin took the book from me and turned it over to read the back. "This one looks good," he said. He sat down on one of the cushy sofas near the wall and set the small stack of books beside him.

"What is it exactly?" I asked. I did my best to shimmy beside him, the way girls in movies do. What's the best way to sit when you want a boy to kiss you? Do you face him? Do you cross your legs?

Why do I feel like I'm going to throw up? Oh God, how do girls know these things?

"Biomimicry is when people study nature to help them figure out problems," he said, flipping through the pages. He pointed to a sketched image of a bird. "See here. People used to study birds to help them find out how to make humans fly," he said.

I leaned over the book, momentarily distracted by the thought. Biomimicry sounded kind of cool. Technically, wasn't my whole "act like a shark" plan against Ashley sort of like biomimicry? Maybe I was a genius like these scientists and didn't even know it.

Only I bet they didn't accidentally put on boy cologne and have shirts that were crusted in old lemonade and Darwin feathers.

"And what do they use it for now?" I asked. I put my arm up on the back of the sofa, trying to subtly lean closer, trying not to focus on the fact that I possibly looked like a bad photoshopped version of myself in this pose.

Kevin sniffed and scratched his nose. "They can use it for all kinds of things," he said. His eyes sparkled. "They can make better buildings, and better medicine, and better cars."

"Wow." I breathed.

Inside, my heart was racing. As he stared at me

with the book in his hands and that half grin he always gave me, I knew I had to try.

Was there an old lady in the sofa across from us reading about quilting? Yep.

Was my stomach churning like I was on a ship in the middle of a stormy sea? Also yes.

Was I scared out of my wits and probably going to faint at any second because *honestly* who *isn't* scared at the thought of actually *kissing* someone for the very first time?

Absolutely.

But still. I couldn't let Liv be the only one to keep our kiss pact. I didn't want to feel like she was miles ahead of me in every single way. I was almost a teenager. *Something* from this summer had to go right. I could do this!

I started to lean toward him, trying to remember every romantic movie I'd ever seen. We weren't outside in the rain or anything like most movies, but a bookstore kiss could be okay. The music seemed to get louder around us as I went for it.

I moved as fast as I could so I wouldn't chicken out. Kevin's eyes widened as I leaned in. I puckered my lips a little. I closed my eyes. I waited for the moment that I'd been picturing for at least three weeks now.

And you know what I did?

I didn't kiss him.

Nope. That would have been too simple. Too perfect.

Instead?

I *head-butted* him.

Why did I head-butt him, you ask?

Because he sneezed.

"Ow!" he yelled, lurching over to cup his nose. "What the—" he said. Blood trickled from under his fingertips. I gasped, jumping up from the sofa.

"Oh no, I'm so sorry!" I said.

He's bleeding. He's bleeding!

"Here, hang on!" I rushed off to the coffee counter, grabbing a pile of napkins. Racing back, I stuffed them into his hand. "This will help," I squeaked. My voice sounded like the time Daz had sucked up helium from the balloons at the fair.

Kevin took the napkins, wadding them up under his nose. There were still angry, red lines dripping from his chin.

"I'm so, *so* sorry," I wailed, mentally cursing my perfume-cologne allergy time bomb. "Do you want some ice? I can get you something! I can get you a frozen hot chocolate from the counter!" I stood there like an idiot, wringing my hands. The old lady with the quilting book had her hand over her mouth, looking as mortified as I did.

He shook his head, waving me off. "No, no, juff gib be a binnit," he said. His words were muffled behind the napkins. "Dun burry. I'be fide." He started toward the door. "Dun wanna beed on de books," he said.

Ten minutes later, the bleeding had finally stopped. We sat on the curb outside the store, with the warm breeze tickling our faces.

If it wasn't for the pile of blood-stained napkins twitching in the breeze *beside* us on the curb, I would have said it was kind of romantic. But nope. On the list of nonromantic things, dirty tissues and head-butting are probably at the top. Right next to parasites.

"Ana," Kevin said for the thirty-fourth time, "it's okay. Really, it was an accident."

"It's not okay, Kev," I said, my voice muffled by my sleeve. "I made you *bleed*."

I stared at my shoes, trying to dig up the courage to even look at him. Did he know I'd been trying to kiss him? Could he see how freaked out I'd been? Did that mean he'd think I was some loser kid who wasn't ready to get a kiss? A million thoughts swam through my head, like an ocean full of angry sharks.

"I do have a question, though," he said. I looked over as the grin spread over his face.

I grimaced. "Yeah?"

"Why the heck do you smell like that?" he asked, sniffing the air.

If I lived to be a hundred, I would always remember this moment and how colossally stupid I felt. This wasn't just regular embarrassment. This was "congratulations-you-get-the-award-for-biggest-screwup-of-all-time" embarrassment. People of the future would probably read *books* about how dumb I was.

"I do reek," I admitted. "I was trying to smell like s'mores. It was kind of an accident."

He snorted. "S'mores?! You think you smell like *s'mores*?!" He looked back at the bookstore. "I'm surprised they haven't issued a warning in there to other customers to watch out for air pollution!"

My shoulders hunched. How had the plan gone so wrong? Not only had I head-butted a guy I liked, but now I *really* had no idea what he was thinking. You can't exactly ask a guy if he likes you after you made him bleed, you know? In fact, pretty much *anything* you have to say after that point is going to sound stupid and wrong. All I wanted to do was disappear.

Or ask that old lady in the bookstore if she needed a quilting buddy, because I sure as heck didn't feel prepared to hang around the opposite sex anymore.

The sound of nothing was deafening.

"Really though. Why did you want to smell like s'mores?" he asked finally.

I bit my lip.

Maybe the least I could do was tell him the truth. On account of the bleeding and all. Or maybe, I didn't have the energy to lie about stuff anymore. My head was heavy and swimmy.

"I was trying to, um." There was no way I could say this. Especially not while he was *staring* at me. I willed the words out of my mouth as I avoided eye contact. "I was trying to kiss you," I said. I let my eyes drift slightly over to him to see his reaction.

He stared ahead into the parking lot. "Oh."

If he was thinking something, it sure as heck wasn't obvious on his blank face. That couldn't be good. Instantly, I wished I'd kept my mouth shut or made up something about having a muscle spasm that had sent me barreling into his face.

His nonreaction made me antsy. "Liv and I had a pact," I blurted. "We wanted to kiss someone before high school. Only I'm not going into high school next year, but *she* is!" I let my head fall into my hands.

Kill. Me. Now.

Kevin shook his head, but his eyes were twinkling. "So she roped you into it," he said. The dimple appeared on his cheek. "Sounds like Liv."

I shrugged. "I guess so? And what do you mean, it sounds like her?"

He crumpled the pile of tissues into a ball and stood up, making his way for the garbage can. "It's just that Liv was always sort of…pushy," he said. "I don't mean that in a bad way. Like, remember that time in fourth grade when Liv wanted to open a dog-sitting business and you wanted to do a snow-cone shop instead?"

I snorted at the memory. Liv and I had spent the whole summer picking up dog poop in her backyard. "Yeah," I said.

"You always went with what she wanted," he explained. "I think it's nice of you, but it always seemed like she sort of…took advantage of it, you know? Like she expected you'd always pick *her* over you."

A small prick of embarrassment niggled away at me. Was it true? Did I always give in to her? When she had mentioned that she was going to high school early, did I actually *say* that I didn't want to go through with the kiss pact? Or had I let her convince me, even though I knew it made me feel all kinds of squiggly wrong inside?

I knew the answer to that.

"I didn't notice," I admitted. I stood up, trying to brush off the dirt from the curb, along with the embarrassment that seemed to cling to me like sticky spiderwebs. Something about what Kevin was saying felt right. Like he had turned a flashlight on inside my head to light up a whole part of my life I'd never thought about. Did that mean Kevin thought I was some weakling then? Someone who couldn't stand up to her friends?

That's not someone I'd want to kiss.

That's not even someone I wanted to *be*.

The wind picked up, and suddenly I felt exposed. Wrapping my arms around myself, all I wanted to do was forget this whole night had ever happened. I wanted to pluck the memory of the head-butting and my stupid confession from Kev's head, so I didn't have to wonder what he thought about me anymore.

I wanted to go back to normal, before kiss pacts and summer bookstore dates were even a thing. I wanted to know if Kevin liked me, but this?

This was like the *worst* way of trying to find out.

Maybe Daz had perfected his time machine by now and I could erase this whole evening? Or better yet, maybe I could zap myself to twenty years old and skip the whole "teenager" thing? So far, the lead-up to it had sucked.

Kevin must have noticed the shift. "Hey, don't worry," he said. "I have an idea."

I sniffed, looking down at my sandals. A few

rogue Nair spots were still healing around my ankle. Another huge Ana fail. "What?" I asked.

He touched his nose, double-checking for blood again. "Let's just forget about the whole thing, okay? We can get out of here and go grab some ice cream or something."

My doubt grew as his words swirled around in my mind.

Forget about the whole thing, like "forget-the-nosebleed-happened-and-have-some-fun-elsewhere-because-maybe-I-like-you-too"? Or forget about the whole thing, like "forget-about-the-kissing-and-let's-go-back-to-normal-and-please-don't-try-to-kiss-me-again-because-I-don't-like-you-that-way-and-this-is-super-awkward"?

Which was it?

And *why* didn't he have anything to say when I told him I was trying to kiss him anyway? Isn't that something you *should* respond to? Or maybe by not saying anything about it, he actually *was* saying something about it?

This night was getting more confusing by the minute, but one thing was for sure: this jumbled mess of feelings inside of me would definitely pair well with a banana split.

"Sure," I said, resigned.

How is it that spending *more* time with someone

can leave you even more confused? Am I just at the tip of the getting-to-date-boys iceberg here? Why do I get the feeling that I'm the only girl in the history of the world that can't figure this stuff out?

Ana's Official Advice for Girls Who Want to Get Their First Kiss without Ruining the Entire Night

1. Do not wear your father's cologne. Even if it comes in a super-girly bottle. And while you're at it, do not try to fix perfume mistakes by adding more perfume. You *cannot undo* perfume. It is like beet juice on a white rug. There is no turning back.
2. If it's on the Internet, it's probably a lie.
3. *Do not head-butt him.*

Chapter 20

The anglerfish has a bioluminescent lure dangling from its face to attract prey.

—*Animal Wisdom*

Can you imagine walking around with that thing? "Oh, hey, Ana! Whoa! What's on your face?!" "Oh, nothing...just my glowing, dangling, weirdo lure!" No wonder those things stick to the bottom of the ocean.

"Everyone ready for the big show today?" Grandpa rubbed his hands together with excitement while Sugar checked her teeth in her spoon. Saturday was turning out to be one of the weirdest days of my life. It was the grand opening of the Adventure

Zone exhibit, and for once, it wasn't *me* doing the presenting. Grandpa and Sugar were back from Los Angeles for the celebration, and because he missed us so much, Grandpa wanted to celebrate with a big family brunch.

Daz helped himself to a massive scoop of eggs, piling them into a mountain on his plate.

"I was born ready," he said, throwing some bacon on top.

Sugar reached over to squeeze my hand. "Well, *I*, for one, cannot wait to see it all put together!" She giggled. "Those sharks, and those cute little jellies, and the sweetheart hermit crabs! People are going to love it!"

I poked at my pancakes. I would have been excited too, if it wasn't for the smarmy thick feeling in the back of my throat. I kept picturing Ashley, getting ready this morning, not even knowing the notebook in her locker was actually *mine*, filled with horrible things. *That image should make me happy, right? So what gives?*

I spread some butter on my pancakes and poured a well of syrup next to my bacon. "Will we get to see you present, Ana doll?" Sugar continued, sipping her orange juice.

I chewed my mouthful of pancakes before answering. "Not this time," I said, keeping my eyes down.

I had the distinct feeling that if I talked too much, my sharky notebook revenge plan would erupt out of me like a volcano of guilt and syrup.

Mom smiled at Sugar. "There's another girl who has been helping out this month," she explained. "Ana has helped her get ready." She lifted her chin proudly.

Hah. "*Helped*" *indeed.*

"Ooh, that sounds like fun!" Sugar said. "It's so sweet of you to help out other kids wanting to learn about all those creatures," she drawled. She handed the ketchup bottle to Dad. "What was the most interesting thing you've learned there?"

"I got one!" Daz piped up, mumbling through his mouthful of bacon. "I learned that a sea cucumber breathes out of its butt!" He cackled.

"Daz…" Dad warned, shaking his head. There was a smudge of syrup next to his mustache. "Don't be disgusting at the table." He wiped his face with a napkin. "Save it for dessert," he added under his breath.

"It's true! They can also make their guts *explode* if they're in trouble!" He smashed his fork into his pile of eggs. "*Ppchhheewww!*" he wailed, making explosion noises. His impression of a sea cucumber was, not surprisingly, pretty disgusting.

Grandpa shook his head and blinked at Mom. "He's not wrong, you know," he acknowledged.

"What about you, kiddo?" Dad asked. "You've

spent more time there than anyone." Everyone at the table turned to me. My fork dropped to my plate with a clang.

"Um." I struggled to think, but only one thing popped into my head. "I liked learning about sharks," I said. "I think it's cool that they're such awesome predators, I mean." I darted a quick look at Dad as my stomach rumbled angrily.

Maybe I had food poisoning. I shoved my plate away, cringing at the sight of my home fries doused in goopy ketchup.

"Hey," I said, looking to Mom. "You guys mind if I excuse myself? I think I'm just nervous for the opening. I'm going to go get some air." I shoved out of my chair and bolted for the bathroom as everyone carried on chattering away about sea cucumbers and hermit crabs.

Alone in the bathroom, I stared at myself in the mirror. I had my trademark ponytail and lime-green zoo shirt on with the sea-blue straps of the new swimsuit I'd gotten with Ashley peeking slightly out of my collar. I looked exactly the same as I did every day.

But I didn't *feel* the same.

I wasn't going to be the one on display today, so why did I feel like a thousand eyes were already watching me?

Forty-five minutes later, the crowd inside the Adventure Zone was packed, and I was having a *serious* case of déjà vu.

People filed through the exhibit, pointing out all the animals and taking pictures next to the life-sized set of great white shark jaws by the door. The horseshoe-shaped tank in the middle of the room was a huge hit, with people bending right down to see the sharks and rays up close. The room looked like a magical marine wonderland come to life, with animals of every color of the rainbow swimming, floating, or scuttling in their tanks.

My heart swelled a teensy bit to see it all. Grandpa had been so right.

Bella and Kevin waved to me from by the door, causing a rush of gratitude to surge through me. Bella had been supersweet about me missing her bake sale, but I knew I didn't deserve it. She was a great friend, and I was going to make sure I tried a *lot* harder to be a better friend to her.

And Kevin? Well, I can't have everything figured out, now can I? He hadn't told Daz about the Great Head-Butting Incident, so I was taking that as a win.

I shoved my way through the growing crowd into

place at the left-hand side of the tank, where Patricia had asked me to be on the lookout for any kids that get too rambunctious for the touch tank while Ashley led her presentation. It was nice for once not to be the center of attention, but I still couldn't stop the grumbly nerves in the pit of my stomach. Was I nervous for Ashley or what?

I shoved the thought down. *Think like a shark, remember?*

Soon, Patricia appeared to rein in the crowd, waving her arms to get everyone's attention.

"Hello and welcome!" she announced. Her usually frizzy hair was tamed for the day, wrangled together in a long braid down her back.

The crowd cheered in response, then quieted again as she spoke. The first few minutes were dedicated to Grandpa, as this whole exhibit was his idea in the first place. Cameras flashed nonstop as he took a bow from the side of the room and gave a little speech with shining eyes. It would have been a cool moment, if I hadn't been so distracted gawking around the room like a jumpy ostrich looking for Ashley.

Where was she?

My question was answered a moment later, when Patricia took the microphone again. "I'm happy to announce that we have a new student volunteer for the Adventure Zone, and she will be leading our marine presentation!" She beamed to the audience, who clapped excitedly.

Ashley appeared beside her, giving the crowd a wave. Another pang of déjà vu swam through me as I remembered the feeling of my own big presentation a couple months ago. The clammy hands. The roiling stomach. The endless sets of eyeballs eagerly waiting for you to mess up.

Was Ashley feeling the exact same way I was back then?

I sucked in a breath as she took the microphone.

She was wearing the green shirt we'd bought at Aviana's together, and her hair had little starfish pins in it. She looked like a star, but it didn't take a genius to see that she was super nervous. Her eyes were blinking double time, and her smile was pinched at the sides even though she was trying to look relaxed.

"Hi, everybody!" she said, her voice sounding strained. The crowd seemed happy to listen to her and were starting to quiet down again.

"Welcome to the new Marine Adventure Zone," she said. She was speaking clearly and slowly now, just right. "As you can see, there are lots of amazing creatures here. Today I'm going to tell you about some of them." She pointed to the surrounding tanks and started to name them for the audience.

She breezed through the moon jellies, the sea horses, and the species in the tide pool, giving the audience an interesting nugget of info about each one.

She was doing a good job, despite the nerves.

The heat in my cheeks began to cool, just a touch.

Then she moved on to the big mangrove tank in front of her, filled with rays and epaulette sharks. "As you can see, these animals are safe to touch, as long as you're very gentle." She demonstrated the proper way to reach into the tank as the little kids in the crowd looked stunned.

"These are epaulette sharks," she said. "They're named that because they have big marks on their shoulders, like they're wearing a military uniform." The audience reacted loudly to the word *shark*, despite the fact that the ones in the tank were smaller and harmless. Ashley didn't miss a beat.

"I know," she said, nodding to the crowd. "When I first started working here, I was afraid of sharks too. I thought they were all nasty man-eaters." She leaned over to stroke one of the sharks in the tank. "But sharks have bad reputations that started years ago. Once you've got a bad reputation, it's hard to get rid of it. Sharks are actually quite harmless, and only a few species have ever hurt people. Really they want to live their lives in peace, like any other animal."

Just then, I felt a strange twinge.

No, it wasn't Nair this time.

It was like two puzzle pieces clicking together in my head. *Ashley had a reputation as a Sneerer, just like sharks had horrible reputations as man-eaters.* Sure, she *was* mean sometimes. And sometimes, she sort of wasn't. Nice people don't call other people "Scales," you know?

But then…technically, don't I call her a "Sneerer"? Which was worse?

I gripped my cold hands together as another dark question grew inside me.

I'd wanted to teach Ashley a lesson by switching the notebooks, but did that mean *I* would start to have a bad reputation too?

Instinctively, I looked to the table set up behind her, searching for the blue notebook. It was there, sitting on top of a pile of books, next to Ashley's bottle of water. Two halves of my brain seemed to be battling each other as I stood there, riveted on that innocent-looking notebook that held some of the worst things I'd ever written.

I *wanted* Ashley to see it because maybe then she'd realize how much of a jerk she was. But what if she did?

That's when the horrible truth hit me: switching the notebooks wasn't acting like a shark. It was acting like a *Sneerer*.

Sharks were just going around being themselves, which *happened* to be sharks. It wasn't like they set out to be mean or steal people's notebooks. No matter *what* Ashley had done to me, being more *like her* was the last thing I wanted to do. In fact, I realized with a pang of regret, I'd practically spent the whole summer trying to deal with everything by acting like *someone else*.

Someone mean.

I hadn't adapted to all these crazy changes at all. I'd just become someone I didn't even want to *be*.

My vision tunneled as the past few weeks came rushing back, forcing me to lean against the wall for support. I wasn't even *sure* if I wanted to kiss Kevin yet, and I had gone ahead and tried to act all aggressive and sharky to do it because of Liv, and what had happened? Head-butting, that's what.

Then I get stuck with Ashley here, and how do I deal with her trying to sabotage me? By acting like a Sneerer!

None of those things are *me*.

The sinking feeling finally settled into my feet, cementing me to the floor. Desperation clawed at me with its tiny, sticky fingers.

Oh no.

Surrounded by dozens of people, shark tanks, and a television crew, my "act like a shark plan" was unraveling by the second, biting me in the butt. My heart hammered in my ears as I checked the table again, with Ashley's voice sounding more and more muffled as I panicked. She still faced the crowd. And she hadn't used the notebook yet or seen my horrible list.

And now I knew the truth: I didn't *want* her to.

I didn't want to be known as a Sneerer. I didn't want to have anything to *do* with mean bullies that ruined people's presentations. I wanted to be *me*, and I might not know everything about what that means, but I *did* know I wasn't a horrible jerk who ruined people's days on purpose.

How had I been such a colossal idiot?!

Tuning out the crowd's commotion, I instantly knew what I had to do.

I snaked through the throng of people directly beside the tank, making my way to the front of the group, next to the gate that opens into the middle of the horseshoe where Ashley was presenting.

It was my only chance: I had to get that notebook before she saw it.

"What do you feed the sharks?" someone piped up, interrupting my mental game plan. I darted a look at Ashley, my heart filling with hope.

She smiled easily. "These sharks eat mostly bottom-feeding invertebrates, like crabs," she said.

"That means animals without backbones," she added quickly.

Yes! Keep on knowing those answers, so I can get that dumb book. I cheered her on in my head.

Reaching my hand around the gate, I felt beneath the inner knob. I could grab the notebook and hide it, and if she happened to not know any of the answers, I would *help* her like a nice person, instead of being a total jerk. She would never know about the notebook, and I could pretend I'd never come up with this whole mess in the first place.

Jimmying the small sliding bolt, my breath caught in my chest.

It was *stuck*.

Patricia must have locked it for real, from the inside, to stop visitors from coming inside during the presentation. *Noooo.*

Dread seized my heart as I peeked up at Ashley again. She was still holding the crowd's attention, but now there were more hands in the air. They were eager to ask her questions, wiggling their fingers to get her to choose them. I prayed to the shark gods they all had super-easy questions. Then a spiky blond head of hair caught my attention at the other end of the horseshoe.

Daz!

He was standing directly across from me on the right side of the tank.

Right beside the gate.

It was the side Patricia and Ashley had entered the tank through, and if they hadn't locked the door coming in, it would still be open. I still had a chance to fix everything.

New hope flickered as I tried to focus all of my attention on Daz. Clenching my fists, I tried to telepathically scream in his mind. We were twins, right? So maybe we had some sort of magical twin ability?

Look at me, Daz! LOOK AT ME!

I crushed my stomach into the gate as I leaned as far in as I could. *Come on, Daz, look up!*

And then, the shark gods paid attention.

He looked!

Well, sort of.

He was actually looking at the teenage girl with the pink dress and flippy ponytail beside me, but eventually I did get his attention.

"Daz!" I mouthed, practically bursting with excitement that my telepathic plan had actually almost worked. "*Dazzzz!*" I tapped the gate erratically.

He cocked his head and lifted his shoulders. Classic Daz "sup?" face.

Forcing as much determination in my eyes as possible, I pointed to Ashley's notebook, miming with my hands opening and closing a book. Around us, the crowd laughed at something Ashley was saying. I stared hard, waiting for Daz to clue in.

Daz glanced at the table, then his eyes widened. "Notebook?" he mouthed. He did the same notebook sign with his hands.

"Grab it!" I mouthed. I mimed yanking something out of the air and holding it to my chest.

Daz screwed up his face, then seemed to get it. "Oh!" He pointed to the book, then to me, and gave me a thumbs-up.

He thought I was telling him I'd switched it. That his *Mission: Impossible*–plan had worked.

Guh.

"No!" I shook my head. "I need it back! Grab it now!" I mouthed the words slowly and clearly as Ashley kept talking over the crowd's excited buzz.

Daz frowned, then pointed to himself. "Me? Grab?" He pointed to the book. I could almost see the question marks floating above his head.

I nodded insistently. "Yes!" I grabbed at my gate and shook it, demonstrating to him my side was locked with a frown.

In a flash, he knew what I wanted. He gave me another quick thumbs-up and reached inside the gate for the lock. Neither Patricia nor Ashley noticed him as they continued with the presentation.

Wringing my hands together, I glanced back out

over the crowd again. Why couldn't the questions stop already?! So far, Ashley had been a total pro and hadn't even needed her notebook. Maybe this would all be fine and she'd never even need to know about my horrible plan?

One final hand was still in the air, a little boy who was waving with excitement.

I sucked in a breath as Ashley pointed. "Last one?"

"Where do the epaulette sharks live?" he asked, scratching at his buzz cut.

I jerked my head back to Ashley, overwhelmed by a surge of relief. An easy one! She knew where everything lived. *She had this!* I bit my lip in anticipation.

But Ashley frowned. Her eyebrows knit together slightly as she blinked at the crowd, silent. Finally, she smirked. "They live right here, of course!"

Nice save.

Boosted by her gutsy move, I stared back at Daz's end of the tank, expecting to see him standing triumphant with the notebook in his hands.

But he was still outside the gate, and instead of a look of victory, his shoulders were slumped with defeat.

My heart fell as he shrugged and shook his head in one slow, sad movement, pointing to the gate.

It was locked too.

This couldn't be happening.

The notebook was still sitting on the table, like

a rattlesnake poised, ready to strike. Terror raced through me as Ashley smiled again at the crowd, edging toward it.

"Hang on one second," Ashley said, returning to the question. "I can tell you!"

She reached toward the table as I clutched the gate, torn between wanting to scream and wishing I could launch myself X-Men style across the fifteen-foot space to wrangle the notebook from her hands.

Why couldn't I be a mutant?!

She picked the notebook up.

The rushing in my head grew like a million bees, swarming with frantic desperation, as her perfectly arched eyebrows furrowed with concentration.

She began to flip open the cover.

No!

I pictured the Anti-Ashley list waiting for her, ready to explode like a mean-girl grenade and ruin everything. All because I was trying to be someone I didn't even *want* to be.

Don't!

I couldn't take it.

My eyes flitted down at the tank. All the sharks were gathered by their mangrove rocks, shying away from the noisy crowd. A reckless thought began to unfurl inside me.

Time slowed to a halt as Ashley's eyes drifted

down to the page. I willed her to drop the book, to sneeze, to stumble—*anything*—to keep her from seeing one those scribbled block letters I wished I could unwrite.

I couldn't let her see it.

I couldn't let this happen.

I couldn't be a Sneerer.

So I jumped.

Or rather, I *dove*.

Leaping over the low wall of the tank, the entire audience scattered back in surprise the moment I hit the water. A giant wave splashed over the edge, raining down on the kids in the front row.

I was a breeching whale, decked out in a lime-green zoo shirt and the most desperate look in the history of mankind. Cameras flashed wildly, and the last image I could make out before my eyes blurred with salt water was the notebook falling to the ground, and Ashley's eyes widening with shock as she saw me.

I'd done it. I'd stopped her. She hadn't seen the notebook.

Then there was nothing but blue.

Well, that and the sharks.

Chapter 21

California sea lions have a thick layer of
blubber to insulate them from cold water.
—*Animal Wisdom*

I never thought I'd say this, but I wish I had
blubber right now. Because shark tank water
was freeeeeezingggg.

"Ana Jane Wright!" Mom's voice sounded like it
was being strained through a can of gravel. "What
in God's green earth were you *thinking*?!"

I pulled the towel closer around me. After
they'd fished me out, pretty much everyone in
the crowd was eager to see that I was still alive.
The crowd watched and hushed whispers filled the

exhibit as Mom dragged me into the back room, while Grandpa stepped into the spotlight to get some of the attention away from us.

It had been only a couple feet of water, but man, that can sure create a splash if you're trying. I'd shooed away the paramedic a hundred times, promising him I was more embarrassed than anything.

And it was true. Being dripping wet in my clothes in front of a crowd of strangers *was* embarrassing. But a part of me was proud I'd done it. Did I wish that maybe I'd thought of something *else* to distract the crowd, like screaming "Fire!" so I *didn't* have to jump into the tank?

Big yes.

But sometimes when you really need it, your brain just decides to check out and you aren't left with a lot of ideas.

Try explaining that to my mom.

"It was an accident!" I pled. But I was pretty sure my mom knew better. She had those special mom powers and could read me like a book.

"I was looking right at you!" she exclaimed. "One minute you were up there watching Ashley looking like you were having a coronary, and the next"—she clapped her hands together hard—"you jumped! I saw you! What would possess you to *jump into a shark tank, young lady?*"

"Mom, stop! It was an accident!" I pulled the towel tighter around my shoulders. "It was only the touch tank. I couldn't have gotten eaten or anything," I pointed out.

She glared at me. "Ana, you have told me the truth about everything in your life so far, and you are *not* going to start lying to me now. Now *spill it*."

Daz shifted on his feet beside her. He had crept in while she was interrogating me, and now he was staring at his shoes and looked as guilty as a monkey in a banana farm. But he wasn't saying anything. I had to hand it to him—he was doing his best to cover for me, even though he knew about the notebook and the truth behind my dip in the tank.

"I…"

Was there any way to get out of this without outing myself as a horrible person? Could I make up something *sort of* true, without telling her the *whole* truth about Ashley and that stupid notebook?

"Um…"

The salt water must have numbed my brain because nothing came to mind. All I could hear was the rushing of water still in my ear. I tapped the side of my head with my palm, trying to shake it out. Ashley stepped through the door and stared at me. Worry was written all over her face. It made telling the truth that much harder.

"I was trying to distract the crowd," I said finally. "I mean, I wanted to get Ashley's attention." I couldn't look her in the eyes.

Mom perched her hands on her hips. "Why exactly would you want to do that? It wasn't your turn to present. It was *Ashley's*," she said. Her eyebrows knit together. "Is that what this is about? You wanted to be the center of attent—"

"No!" I said. "Honestly, it wasn't! I was trying to help her." Ashley's head cocked as she listened, doing her best to look like she wasn't. Her cheeks were red.

There was no way out of this.

"Help her by jumping into a shark tank? Ana, you could have been *hurt*! You know that the circumstances when you're allowed near the touch tank are very specific, and if you don't respect that, *you can be hurt*!" She was still wringing her hat in her hands, twisting the fabric.

"I know!" I said. "I didn't think of that. But I really did want to help her. She had the wrong notebook…" I trailed off.

Ashley's lips pressed together tight as she listened.

"She was only going to use her notes to help her—" Mom stopped short, turning the full force of her glare onto me. I shriveled down in my chair.

"Wait. *What did you do?* What do you mean the *wrong* notebook?"

Pretty sure her eyes were burning a hole in my forehead now. Humiliation spread over me again. I didn't want to face it. But I was done being a wimp. I'd spent too long trying to be someone else, changing who I was to adapt to scary stuff in my life. If I wanted to be confident, if I really wanted to be *myself*, I would *own* the fact that I had been a super jerk, even if it was momentarily. That felt crummy, but I had the sneaking feeling it would be the closest thing to brave I'd been since summer started.

I glanced up at Ashley. My skin felt pinched from the salt water, but I was pretty sure it was because I was shrinking down to nothing. I wanted to disappear.

You have to be brave now.

"It wasn't supposed to happen," I said quickly. "I switched our notebooks, and then—" I sucked in a breath. Mom's reaction made me wince.

"I realized it was a horrible, *mean* idea!" I rushed on. "It wasn't me. I mean, I know it *was* technically me. But not really." I struggled for the right words. Mom's glare darkened as my story unfolded. Saying it out loud made it sound ridiculously dumb. "Obviously I was a gigantic jerk."

I stared at my sopping wet shoes, but Mom wasn't letting me get away that easy.

"And…"

"And when I saw you were about to read it, I got…I panicked," I said, turning to Ashley.

Understanding finally dawned on Mom's face. Her shoulders drooped. Shame crawled over my skin like a centipede.

"What was in the book, Ana?" she said in a low voice.

I shrugged. "Just some mean stuff I'd written." I couldn't speak above a whisper. "I was so angry!" A prick of tears tickled behind my eyes. Ashley was still staring at me with a tight frown.

"Since when do you behave in such a vicious way?" Mom said coldly.

The words sliced through me like knives. I knew it was true. I'd probably known it all along. But I especially didn't want to hear it out loud coming from her. That made it real, and already I wanted to put that person behind me and bury her in a note-book that never got opened again.

"I know," I said. "It was a dumb idea."

The lines around Mom's mouth seemed deeper than normal.

"Ana…that is *appalling*," she said.

"I know! That's why I had to stop it from happening! I messed up before. I know that! I *did* try to fix things. Only I didn't know how!" I said. "All I could think of was to jump into the tank when I saw she was going to see it!"

Mom sank down onto the bench, like her legs were noodles. For a moment, she looked like she was going to yell at me again. She rubbed her temples with her fingertips. Clocks around the world stopped.

"You do realize you're grounded right?" she said finally.

I nodded.

"And you should never *ever* do something so mean again, no matter how much you don't like someone?"

I nodded again.

"And next time, maybe don't pick the shark tank as a distraction."

"Yes, Mom," I said.

"I'm proud of you," she said. I peeked up at her.

Mom kneeled in front of me and gripped me by the shoulders. "You're in huge trouble, kiddo. But I'm proud of you. You made a big mistake, but you tried to make it right in the end. I think you owe Ashley an apology." She stroked the wet hair from my face and tucked it behind my ear.

"I know," I mumbled. I had a feeling this was coming, but that didn't make facing her any easier. Mom dragged Daz out of the room, but not before she shoved me in Ashley's direction.

"Be honest," she whispered hastily.

Ashley stepped forward.

"So," Ashley said. Her mouth was turned up in a

look of disgust. But could I blame her? "You wrote a whole book about why you hate me, huh?" she said plainly.

I forced myself to look at her. This was worse than facing a shark any day. "I'm really sorry, Ashley," I said. "I didn't want you to see it. I was super angry, and I thought being like that would fix things. I didn't know what else to do to get you back."

She gave a small snort. "No kidding. Get back at me for what?"

I tried not to sound mean. I just wanted to tell her the truth. "For making it look like I left that lock open," I said. "I mean, I know why you did it. I shouldn't have said that awful stuff about you. I was upset too." I let the words tumble out fast. "I was mad at you for doing that, and then I got *really* upset when Patricia blamed me for it, and well... that really sucked."

Ashley's eyes widened. "Ana, I keep telling you. I *didn't* leave the lock open," she said.

I blinked at her. "Seriously, Ashley, it's okay. I'm not mad, and like I said, I was wrong. I never should have done that, and it was my fault for being such a jerk that Patricia kicked me out."

"No! I mean it! I swear." Her hand flew to her chest. "On my best pair of jeans, I did *not* leave that door unlocked."

My jaw dropped. "But my name was scrubbed off the list!" I said. "And I *know* I had it coming, I—"

A loud commotion echoed outside the door, cutting me off. Men yelling. A woman shrieking.

Ashley's head whipped around. "What the—?"

Chapter 22

Barracudas are capable of swimming at
speeds of twenty-five miles an hour.

—Animal Wisdom

Ashley and I shoved the door open just in time to
see Danielle, Logan's perfectly perky and porcelain-
skinned girlfriend, being marched away by two zoo
security guards.

"Right this way, miss!" the guard said in a deep
voice, while another held open the door for them.
But Danielle wasn't having it. She yanked herself
away from him, stumbling through the crowd,
trying to get away.

"Let me go right *now*, you jerk! I didn't do anything! You have no right!" she wailed. In the throes
of yelling her head off, I have to say: she didn't seem
that glamorous anymore.

Beside me, Ashley gripped my arm. "Oh my God!" she hissed. "I *told* you that girl was trouble! I wonder what happened?!" She giggled and gave me a sneaky grin of satisfaction. We both took a few steps closer to better hear what was going on.

The guard shook his head, getting a grip on Danielle's arm. "Enough, miss. Ma'am, we've got her." Danielle seemed to realize that struggling was creating more of a scene. Instead, she glared angrily as the guard steered her out.

Patricia nodded solemnly at the door. "That's her. She was in here last night, fiddling with the locks," she said.

I watched in awe as the two guards escorted Danielle out the door, navigating through the zoo visitors. It was the first time I'd ever seen someone in trouble with the police, and I have to admit, the whole thing was a little thrilling.

"What happened?" Ashley dragged me over to Patricia. Now that Danielle was out of there, everyone seemed to be pretty amused by the whole thing. Eye rolls and embarrassed smiles filled the room, and people went back to leaning over the shark tank and exploring the tide pool. To them, it was an exciting day at the zoo.

Patricia wrapped her arm around me. "Shep told me that we had cameras installed to document the exhibit being built. Guess who we saw unlocking the crabs when I checked the tapes?" She shook her head, disappointed.

"Danielle?!" I said. I darted a look at Ashley. "Why would she do that?"

Patricia's eyebrows narrowed. "It seems she's working on a little *exposé* of zoos for her college newspaper. Logan said she wasn't finding a good story here apparently, so she thought she'd create one. He caught her in the back rooms alone earlier and got suspicious, then came to me once he figured out what was going on."

Ashley glared at me, but it was more of a playful "I *told* you so, dimwit" glare, rather than a "you totally suck" glare.

Patricia's face reddened. "I'm sorry, Ana. I know I blamed you for this, and I shouldn't have. The police asked me not to say anything until we had apprehended her. We could have saved a lot of heartache for you, but Logan was positive she would show up today after I showed him the footage." She squeezed my shoulder.

"It's okay. I deserved it. I shouldn't have blamed Ashley either." I was starting to notice that the more I admitted this horrible truth, the easier it was.

"It's been an exciting day, girls," Patricia said. "You should go and enjoy the rest of it! And, Ana, you need a shower. You smell like shark food," she joked, pinching her nose together.

"Well, that's nothing new," Ashley quipped as Patricia hustled back inside.

"So," Ashley said, leaning against the outer wall of the Adventure Zone. She leaned her head back, sunning herself for a moment. "I have a question."

"Yeah?" I asked. I rubbed my hair with a towel and tried to get the last of the shark water from my ear.

"You said you thought I unlocked that door to sabotage you."

I winced. "Yeah. I did. It was stupid, I know."

"No, it's not that. I'm just wondering." She bit her lip. "Why would you jump into the tank then? If you thought I did that to you, *why* wouldn't you let me read your dumb book, then? You had no way of knowing it was Danielle…"

I nodded. "Even if it *was* you, I didn't want to ruin your presentation. I might have even deserved it," I said.

"I don't get it." Her face softened a notch.

"All this time I've been thinking you've been a jerk to me for years. And yeah, you sort of have been." I tugged at the hem of my damp shirt, wringing out some of the water. "But I wasn't seeing that I'd also been a huge jerk to you. I'm sorry about the whole crocodile thing," I said. "At my first presentation, I mean. I shouldn't have grabbed you from the crowd. I'm sorry you got embarrassed."

I hesitated. There was something else. I didn't want to miss this chance again. "And I'm sorry I call you a Sneerer," I said. "I have no idea when I started that, but I'm sorry."

She curled her lip. "I probably deserved it too."

"Honestly, that's why I thought you were here in the first place. To get revenge on me for how I embarrassed you in that presentation!"

Her eyes dropped, suddenly glistening with what looked an awful lot like tears.

"What is it?" I asked.

She straightened her shoulders, and the fiery look returned to her face. "I'm here because I didn't have a choice."

"What do you mean?" I asked.

"My parents saw your presentation that day," she said. "At the end of school, I mean. They wanted me to be *confident* like you and said this would be a great place to do it. They wouldn't take no for an answer," she explained. "They said I could learn a lot from this place. And from you." She tried to smile, but it got lost in her eyes.

I swallowed hard as she hastily swiped at her eyes with the back of her hand. I didn't know what to say. I was proud, I guess. If Ashley's parents thought I was cool enough to be around, then that was good, right?

But a big part of me was sad. I couldn't imagine my mom telling me to be more like some other kid. That would make me feel rotten.

More than rotten. I'd just spent the summer *trying* to be someone I'm not and hating every minute of it, and here Ashley's parents were encouraging it?

"I'm sorry," I said. "For what it's worth, you're pretty much *the* most confident person I know, so..." I wanted to boost her up a little but had the feeling there was a lot about Ashley that I still didn't understand.

She shrugged, facing me again. "I've had fun here. I didn't think I would. Especially when Brooke and Rayna took off for the summer. I thought it would be smelly and weird," she said. "Like you!" She smirked, but it wasn't long until her face dissolved back into a genuine smile. "But it was seriously great."

"I'm glad."

"Your brother is insane," Ashley added, swiveling her head to watch Daz file out of the Adventure Zone after Bella. He had a stuffed octopus on his head.

"You know," I said, "that is something we will always agree on."

Her eyes darted behind me. "Um, I have to go,"

she said suddenly. She brushed off her shirt and started to walk away.

I blinked. "What? Why don't we hang out or something?"

But Ashley shook her head and gave me a pointed look. "Maybe later," she said. On her way brushing past me, she whispered, "Fluff your hair up."

I gulped, whipping my hands to my hair.

There was only one person it could be.

I tried to look calm and collected as Kevin peeked around the sign to find me. For the record, it's hard to act like you're surprised to see someone when you've secretly spent the past fifteen seconds trying not to look like a drowned mop *for* them.

"Nice presentation," he said, gesturing inside the exhibit. He settled against the wall, keeping a couple feet between us. Already my mind was spinning, trying to guess his thoughts. Did he think I was an even bigger fool now? Did he forgive me for the head-butting?

"I just wanted to make sure you were okay," he said.

I grimaced. "Oh, you know. I felt like a swim, that's all." I tried to act nonchalant, but with the dripping water everywhere, it was pretty hard to pull off.

His mouth quirked into a smile. "So I was thinking," he said. "About that kiss…"

My heart began to pound. "Oh yeah?"

What do I do? What do I say?

"You really caught me off guard with the whole… uh, nosebleed thing." He fiddled with his hands as he spoke, picking at his thumbnail. "I know it was Liv's idea, and I don't know if you actually *wanted* to…"

I cringed. I didn't want to talk about that horrible nosebleed incident ever again, but especially not when I had overcooked spaghetti hair and reeked of sharks.

"But if you do want to, I mean…" He looked around nervously. "We can if you want." His eyes brightened as he turned to face me. His cheeks were bright red. "I mean, what guy wouldn't want to kiss the girl who was brave enough to swim with sharks?"

My jaw dropped. Did he just say what I think he said?! I replayed every word, making sure I hadn't heard them in the wrong order or something because of the shark water in my ears.

OH MY GOD. BE COOL. BE COOL.

I couldn't stop myself from beaming. *He wanted to kiss me.* The words skipped through my head like a pixie on a sugar rush. "It was hardly swimming," I joked. "More like floundering pathetically."

I gave myself a million points for getting that sentence out without completely flipping from excitement. If I wasn't going out of my way to stand still, I would have been jumping for joy in a super-embarrassing victory dance right now.

He nodded. "I'm glad you're okay. Like I said, I wanted you to know." He brushed his hair from his eyes and gave me that funny little grin of his.

I smiled back, but despite how amazing it was to hear it, something about this didn't feel right. And after the summer I'd had, I was getting a little too used to that feeling.

A strange calm settled over me as I realized what felt so off. I didn't want to let Liv decide when I had my first kiss.

Or my first *anything*.

"You know what?" I said. "If it's okay with you, I'd rather not have my first kiss covered in shark water and smelling like fish," I said, letting out my breath.

For the first time I wasn't worried what he would think. I wasn't worried about Liv, who was probably going to get her first kiss any moment with that Ryan guy in the movie theater, and I wasn't worried about any stupid pact.

I knew what *I* wanted. I wanted to be me, and I wanted to kiss Kevin when I was good and ready.

And ideally without shark poop up my nose or anything.

Kevin laughed. "Yet you're fine with smelling like a perfume explosion."

I nudged him with my shoulder, leaving a wet mark on his shirt. "I know. I messed up a lot of things this summer. I don't want my first kiss to be one of them, I guess."

"I like you, Ana," he said softly. "You're an absolute *nutcase*. But I like you. I just thought you should know that, in case you're wondering. I know I was," he said, kicking at the dirt. "I mean, before the whole bookstore thing," he added.

A hot blush of embarrassment washed over me, as I remembered how much I'd tried to change this summer. To get kissed for the kiss pact. To seem cool in front of Logan. But with Kevin, I didn't need to do any of that.

I could just be me.

"And whenever *you* want to kiss? I'm okay with that." He stared at a bird perched on a picnic table in front of us, pecking away at some abandoned fries. "Just don't head-butt me or anything, okay?" His eyebrows lifted hopefully.

Now *I* was definitely blushing.

"I like you too," I said.

Yep, my face was definitely boiling.

I know it wasn't kissing, but hearing Kevin say he liked me was probably *the* coolest thing ever. It was better than a kiss right now because it was *real* and not forced and only him and me without anybody else mucking it up. I wanted to take this moment and put it in a jar and keep it forever, so I could pull it out and relive it a thousand times over.

"I should go," he said, glancing back toward the door. "Your folks are waiting for you inside. See you at dinner tonight? They invited me out with your grandpa and Sugar." He stood up and flashed me his very best dimply smile.

"For sure," I said, tucking my towel closer. "See you later."

He waved good-bye, and I watched as he walked away from the Adventure Zone, disappearing from view.

And you know what?

I'd *love* to say that I kept my cool and was all sophisticated and chill when he was gone. But I was done trying to be something I wasn't.

The truth is, the moment Kev was out of sight, I collapsed into a pile of squealing happiness and spazzy giggles like an absolute loon, right next to the sign about great white shark anatomy.

Some things never change, right?

Top Three Coolest Things about This Summer

1. Kevin. Because OH MY GOD. He likes me. HE LIKES ME! And who cares if I didn't kiss him yet?! Because HE LIKES MEEEE.

2. Ashley. I know. I never saw it coming either. But she's seriously cool and can pick a swimsuit like a pro too.
3. Daz. Possibly the biggest surprise of all. But he really came through for me, and it wasn't his fault he couldn't get that gate open. Is it possible my brother's been replaced by an actual...*human*?

Chapter 23

Despite its size, the manta ray is a harmless filter feeder with no teeth.

—*Animal Wisdom*

This makes me wonder what else seems super scary but is actually harmless. Do you think eighth grade seems worse than it really is?

T-minus fourteen minutes until school starts.

Sometimes, it hits me that I'm almost friends with Ashley. Well, not even *almost*.

Turns out that jumping into a shark tank to save someone's feelings can make friends out of enemies.

CREATURE FILE—REVISED EDITION!

SPECIES NAME: Ashleydae Reignus Ashleydae Surprisia

KINGDOM: Pretty much wherever she is, she owns it.

PHYLUM: People Who Turn Out Not-so-Bad After All; (still an apex member of Swim Team Goddesses, though.)

WEIGHT: Yep, still perfect.

NATURAL HABITAT: I'm sure she still likes all the same places as before, but I bet you can add the Marine Adventure Zone to this list! She even became an official "zoo ambassador" for the rest of the year!

FEEDS ON: Shopping trips (don't forget the squat test), burritos, books about sharks (who knew?!), shiny lip gloss, and surprisingly corny jokes.

LIFE SPAN: previous calculation of witchlike immortality likely wrong; turns out she's a human like the rest of us.

HANDLING TECHNIQUE: Only bites when backed into a corner. Can also be bribed with pictures of Logan in a wetsuit.

NOTES ASHLEYDAE SURPRISIA CAN ALWAYS BE DEPENDED UPON FOR WARDROBE

CHECKS, EXTRA LIP GLOSS, TOUGH LOVE PEP
TALKS, AND TOKEN EYE ROLLS WHEN YOU'RE
ACTING LIKE A BIT OF A TURD.

To anyone watching, we might have been friends for years. I mean, sure, there are times when I look at her and roll my eyes because she says something that sounds shallow. I don't think she even means to sound that way. It's just hard to kick the habit of noticing it. But there are also times where she gives me *a look* because I'm being super nerdy or talking about elephant poop.

But my other friends do that too.

Even my own *brother* does that.

I used to always think that friends were something you found when you were younger, and you got closer as you got older together. You either had them, or you didn't. Like with Liv. I always thought because we were best friends, there wasn't room for new friends, especially ones that were formally known as "Sneerers." And yeah, she still does sneer sometimes, but I'm not about to call her that. I sneer too after all.

Because she does a lot more than sneer too, you know?

I stared up at the building and tried to swallow my fear. "I don't know if I'm ready for this," I said. "Eighth grade now." I straightened my shirt and tried to mimic Ashley, who was standing tall. "That's kind of a big deal."

"That's right." She grinned. Her hair was glossy and waving in the breeze. "It's going to be *awesome*."

I thought about Liv, who would be starting her first day of high school soon. I didn't feel as confident as her—that was for sure. And I definitely didn't feel as confident as Ashley, who was slapping on another coat of lipstick. The other Sneerers—*no*—her other *friends*, Brooke and Rayna, weren't here yet. I wasn't sure what would happen once school started and Ashley reunited with her old friends.

But I wasn't as scared to find out now.

"Let's go, Scales." She pulled me toward the door.

"Hey, wait a minute! We promised no more name-calling!" I pulled myself away from her.

She grinned sneakily. "Whatever. You'll always be Scales to me. Get over it." She rolled her eyes, and for a brief moment I saw the old Ashley, ready to attack.

I stepped back, my mouth hanging open. "Seriously! After everything, you can't even be nice for two seconds and—"

"I'm *kidding*, Ana!" she scoffed. "You look cute today, by the way. Your butt especially. That skirt is killer."

"Hey, guys!" Bella ran up to us, with Daz and Kevin following behind her. Daz was carrying a stack of atlases, and Kevin's hair had been freshly cut for school.

He smiled shyly at me. "Hey, Ana." My heart fluttered like a hummingbird as he laced his fingers between mine. He didn't even care that Daz was looking! It wasn't a kiss, but that made it even more perfect. You know how when you go to the movies and you're sitting there in the seat, eating your popcorn, and the lights suddenly dim and the sound gets super loud and you get this awesome sense of *here we go* because you can't *wait* to see this great movie?

That's how I felt when Kevin held my hand. Like I was excited and nervous and eager and everything all at the same time. Luckily I wasn't a total freak and didn't actually *say* this, because *hello, mortifying*. But he could probably tell by the way I squeezed his hand back that I was feeling it, though.

"Hey," Ashley said, snapping me out of my dreamy delirium. She turned to Bella. "You're Bella, right?"

I held my breath, waiting to see how Bella would react. I still wasn't sure how to navigate having friends from totally different circles. It sort of felt like worlds colliding, bashing into each other. I was afraid something was going to explode or catch fire or cause some sort of social earthquake. Bella and I were fine now, but asking her to handle someone like Ashley might be too much.

But I didn't have to worry.

Bella grinned. "Yup. I've got Mrs. Randall first period. How 'bout you guys?" She read from her class schedule, which she'd printed and laminated.

Ashley nodded. "Me too!" She tucked her lipstick into her purse and shook out her hair. "Let's go before the good seats are taken."

She marched ahead, then turned around to stare at me. "You coming or what?"

BELLA'S (ALMOST) HEALTHY NO-BAKE COOKIES

It's summertime, right? So there's no way you want to be heating up your house with a hot oven for ages. This is Bella's best recipe for no-bake cookies. At least, *I* think they're the best, and I'm pretty sure Daz agrees because he ate half the batter before we even had a chance to finish.

Enjoy!

STUFF YOU'LL NEED:

- -1/2 cup of some kind of nut butter (I like crunchy peanut butter, but if you're allergic, you can substitute in whatever kind you like!)
- -1/4 cup butter
- -1/3 cup honey
- -1 cup of oats (make sure you get the "quick cook" flake kind, **not** the "steel-cut" kind)
- -1/2 cup unsweetened coconut

-1/2 cup dried fruit (my favorite is dried cranberries, but you can also use raisins, chopped dried apples, or even dried cherries)

-1/2 cup of chocolate chips (the best part)

-2 tablespoons of ground flaxseed (optional, but super healthy!)

-nonstick cooking spray

-a small pot

-a clean drinking glass

-a cookie sheet

-waxed paper

-spoons

WHAT TO DO:

1. With a grown-up's help if you need it, start by melting the nut butter, butter, and honey in a small pot. You only need to have the heat on low for this, but make sure you don't burn yourself! Stir it all up with a spatula until its smooth.

2. Remove the pot and turn off the stove. Add in the remaining ingredients, stirring the whole thing together until it looks like a gloopy, sticky mess. This is normal!

3. Layer a cookie sheet with the wax paper. Now use your spoons to scoop globs of batter into mounds on the sheet. I like to make them about the size of a golf ball, but if you want bigger cookies, that's okay too. Do this with all the batter.

4. Once you've filled up your cookie sheet, spray the bottom of a clean drinking glass with nonstick cooking spray. Very *carefully* squish each glob flat with the glass, until it's about 1/2-inch thick. They will look like cookies now!

5. When you've flattened all the globs, stick the whole cookie sheet into the fridge. It will take them about an hour to set, so distract yourself. Or if you're like Daz, wait four minutes and steal them from the fridge early. Either way, they taste great!

Acknowledgments

As always, this one goes out to Kathleen Rushall. Every book I write may be different, yet the one thing that doesn't change is how incredibly grateful I am to have you as my brilliant agent and partner-in-crime. You're the best!

To Aubrey Poole, Jillian Bergsma, Kathryn Lynch, Rachel Gilmer, and everyone behind the scenes at Sourcebooks—your enthusiasm, keen eyes, and hard work never go unnoticed and I hope you know how much I appreciate everything you've done to get these books out into the world.

To the Nerdy Book Club, and the amazing kidlit community! I can't thank you enough for welcoming Ana and the gang with open arms, and supporting books and literacy at every turn. Your tweets, emails, letters, and blogs are a writer's dream. I've always said that book people are some of the most generous, spirited, and thoughtful people around, and you prove me right every day!

To my awesome parents and family, for a lifetime of love, support, and full bookshelves.

To Carter, Alina, Lauren, Julie, Liv, Adrienne, and Josh, as well as my amazing #TeamKrush buddies! You all inspire me, and I'd be lost (and likely very bored!) without you.

To Justin, for being an awesome husband and best friend.

And once again, to my wonderful readers! Thank you for taking Ana's adventures and bringing them to life in your minds and hearts. I hope she inspires you to let your true selves shine.

About the Author

Jess Keating was nine years old when she brought home a fox skeleton she found in the woods and declared herself Jane Goodall, and not much has changed since then. Her first job was at a wildlife rehabilitation center, where she spent her days chasing raccoons, feeding raptors (the birds, not the dinosaurs!), and trying unsuccessfully to avoid getting sprayed by skunks. Her love of animals carried her through university, where she studied zoology and received a Master's degree in Animal Science, before realizing her lifelong dream of writing a book for kids about a hilarious girl who lives in a zoo.

She has always been passionate about three things: writing, animals, and education. Today, she's lucky enough to mix together all three. When she's not writing books for adventurous and funny kids, she's hiking the trails near her Ontario home, watching documentaries, and talking about weird animal facts* to anyone who will listen. You can email her at jesskeatingbooks@gmail.com, or visit her online at www.jesskeating.com.

*Did you know a blue whale's tongue can weigh as much as an elephant?

CREATURE FILE:
Jess Keating

SPECIES NAME: Authorificus Biophiliac

KINGDOM: Ontario, Canada!

PHYLUM: Writers who have a strange love of quirky critters and brave characters; Animal nut with a pen

WEIGHT: You dare ask a lady her weight?! Why, I never! Wait, is this before or after I ate that banana split?

NATURAL HABITAT: Outside exploring with a messy notebook, or snuggled up watching nature documentaries with her husband.

FEEDS ON: Grilled apple and cheese sandwiches, popcorn, and pizza.

LIFE SPAN: I was born on a sunny summer day in... wait, nobody has time for my life story here. Get it together, Jess.

HANDLING TECHNIQUE: Gets restless inside, so daily walks are essential. Also have significant quantities of caramel corn and extra books on hand in case of emergency.

How to Outrun a Crocodile When Your Shoes Are Untied

Jess Keating

Ana Wright's social life is now officially on the endangered list: she lives in a zoo (umm, elephant droppings!?), her best friend lives on the other side of the world, and the Sneerers are making junior high miserable. All Ana wants is to fade into the background.

Yeah, that's not going to happen.

Coming Soon:

HOW TO OUTFOX YOUR FRIENDS WHEN YOU DON'T HAVE A CLUE

October 2015